DEATH

IN THE

THIRD ACT

DEATH

IN THE

THIRD ACT

by

John Scherber

The Nineteenth Book in the Murder in Mexico
Series

San Miguel Allende Books

San Miguel de Allende, Guanajuato, Mexico

ACKNOWLEDGMENTS

Any book starts as one person's idea and finishes by being a group effort. I am most grateful to the following:

The theater people of San Miguel de Allende, México, who took the time to coach me in theater lore and to share their experience with me: Clara Dunham, Michael Alton Gottlieb, and Jim Newell. Any errors or misrepresentations are entirely my own.

To Captain Neil Low of The Seattle Police Department.
To my wife, Kristine Scherber, for editorial and critical help.
Lander Rodriguez for the cover design.
Julio Mendez for website design.

ISBN 978-0-9906551-7-6

San Miguel Allende Books
www.sanmiguelallendebooks.com

Also by John Scherber

FICTION

(The Paul Zacher Murder in México mystery series)

Twenty Centavos

The Fifth Codex

Brushwork

Daddy's Girl

Strike Zone

Vanishing Act

Jack and Jill

Identity Crisis

The Theft of the Virgin

The Book Doctor

The Predator

The Girl from Veracruz

Angel Face

Uneasy Rider

Lost in Chiapas

The Jericho Journals

Noble Rot

Twilight at Tikal

If it is shown in the first act that a rifle is hanging on the wall, in the second or third act it absolutely must be fired.

–Anton Chekhov

The primary task of art is to illuminate and comment on life, but if art precisely mirrored life we wouldn't need it.

--Derek Hamilton, *A Philosophy for Our Time*

For Kristine

CHAPTER ONE

Now and then I hear about some lucky person getting The Call. Usually it's an actor landing the stage or movie role of a lifetime, paired with an established leading man or actress, or a musician being invited to go on tour as the front act to a big star, a position that will jumpstart his career. It's always a life-changing moment.

In the first five or six years I was painting, into my mid twenties, I used to dream about getting The Call too. The phone would ring one morning as I sat at my easel and on the other end would be the voice of the assistant to the curator of painting at the Museum of Modern Art.

"Do you have, Mr. Zacher," she would say, after introducing herself in a cultured voice, "a set of images of your available recent work that you could email to us so we can select three pictures of yours to include in a group show? We're going to call it *Up and Coming Painters in America: How the Future Looks from Here*. We've heard so much about you recently in New York." This made me wonder whether she knew I lived in México, but I would say nothing about that. I had moved to San Miguel right after college.

Then my partner Maya Sanchez would come in so she could help me up off the floor of my studio. Except that Maya and I weren't yet a couple back then.

Later on, in my dual career as a detective at the Paul Zacher Agency and still a painter, it was always clear that it would be the painter who got The Call if one ever came. Detectives don't get calls like that. Detectives get calls when their dry cleaning is ready or their oil change is finished. Too often it's a wrong number at three A.M. when somebody's husband didn't make it back from the local bar. None of these paths lead to glory, and few even lead to satisfaction.

I was ruminating about this as the three of us that comprise The Paul Zacher Agency were all sitting front row center in the San Miguel Play House on Avenida Independencia in San Miguel de Allende, México. Maya was on my right, and our partner in the Agency, Cody Williams, was on my left. We were there because I had gotten The Call ten months before. It was not quite in the same league as the summons to artistic glory from the Museum of Modern Art. In fact, The Call had come in for me as a *detective* after all.

"Did you see the photo of the actor they've got

playing me tonight?" Maya said closely against my ear. She gripped the playbill in her right hand. "I think she's *older* than I am! She could be thirty-five. Maybe even thirty-six." Maya was thirty and we had been together for nine years. Her figure was graceful and flexible. In fact, she had posed nude for me in more than forty pictures, now widely dispersed from Calgary to Quito. "They could've picked someone twenty-four to play me, you know? Like I would be an ingénue. And besides, this woman doesn't even look Mexican!"

"Actors don't always play their exact age or ethnic background," I said in an undertone, "although I'm sure the director wants them to be close whenever that's possible. What if she's intelligent and perceptive, with a real knack for languages, and occasional bouts of snorkiness? Wouldn't that be a good fit for you? That's what acting is all about. I'm sure she'll be fine, since they cast her based on her skills. Her task will be to reach into her psyche and her depth of experience and come up with a plausible version of you."

"Good luck with that," she said with a flip of her hair. Maya's English was nearly perfect and she had given extensive study to American slang.

"Anyway, young actors must be hard to find here." The San Miguel expat population of around ten thousand was mostly retired in an active way, but there were few Americans or Canadians still in their twenties.

And fewer still of those were actors.

This also raised the question of who would be playing me. I'd find out soon enough. Hopefully it wouldn't be some dwarflike character actor with elevator shoes and taller ambitions. I'm a fraction over six feet and loose in build, and I turned forty earlier this year. The photo of the actor in the program was only a head shot, so while he was about the right age, possessed of sufficient maturity, and good looking with excellent teeth, it didn't tell me much more. His name was Lance Bitman.

Our partner, Cody Williams, presented his own casting problem. I could imagine the audition call that went out for him. He was six-foot-three and weighed around 230 pounds. He'd spent thirty years on the homicide squad in Peoria before he moved to San Miguel at retirement in his late fifties. Over the thirty years of his stint on that beat he'd been shot four times, but if that came up onstage the scars could be faked with makeup. The photo in the playbill of the actor cast as Cody showed a man in his fifties with a wide face, but you couldn't tell much more.

The Call I'd received in this instance came from the theater where we were seated that evening, attending the debut of a new play. It came from Ken Fairfax, the theater manager, an actor with decades of experience, and the director of this production. He told me they had become part of an educational project with a young bilingual Mexican MFA student at the University of Guanajuato, a campus in our capital city known mainly for law and theater studies, a combination that may not have been as odd as it looked at first glance. Especially for law students planning a career in litigation or criminal defense. The student's name was Rodrigo Ferrer.

Ken told me Ferrer's master's thesis required him to write a detective play in English and have it produced. The San Miguel Play House was going to host and assist the production for a three-night run, although Ferrer would be bringing in support people from among his peers, faculty, and friends to serve as stage manager, prop mistress, several roles onstage, and similar tasks. Ken Fairfax was going to mentor the project as well as directing. I had known him for several years, but not well. While he was a serious person in theater matters, his easy sense of humor lay not far below the surface.

"That sounds exciting," I said to him on that first call, in a measured tone, "but I'm not sure how I could help you with it. Are you looking for consultation on detective procedures? Because our partner, Cody Williams, would be the one for doing it by the book, American style. Maya and I rely more on improvisation."

Ken went on to explain. He asked if I had on file good records of all our cases (there had been eighteen of them by that time), and would I be willing to allow

Rodrigo Ferrer to review them, select one, and dramatize it? Since he had lived in the States for eight years before coming back to México for college, he was confident of his English writing skills to dramatize the action, but for credibility, he felt he needed a genuine case to build the plot around, and he didn't know much detail of how a real detective agency operated.

In fact, I could do that, I told Ken, since all my case notes were accurate and complete from the beginning. To some degree these outings represented solid efforts that sometimes achieved only a mixed level of success. That meant the files were realistic about the challenges detectives face in this kind of boutique agency, and they were always honest about what hadn't worked, because we wanted to learn from them ourselves. Maya and Cody, hearing this with tiny stars dancing in their eyes, had no objection, either. Of course, we insisted that all the client and suspect names be changed in the play, even those of the people who hadn't survived.

Although the direct benefit to our detective agency business was not obvious, it did sound like fun, even if part of that was merely the vanity of watching a number of skillful people, well practiced in pretending to be other people, prancing around on stage simulating the three of us—or more likely, simulating a group of detectives more intelligent and skillful than we'd ever really been, but still more interesting to the audience. To do this would illustrate what kind of magic the theater was able to provide, since we knew the raw material better than anyone else could.

Within two weeks Rodrigo Ferrer, a personable and very polite young man of twenty-three, had chosen his favorite case from our files and was hard at work to make it, as he must've thought, come alive as a drama. While these cases had often been more dramatic to us than we wished, and leaning far more often toward tragedy than comedy, still, there were many ways for him to do this that we hadn't thought of when the cases originally played out. I couldn't help but notice that he especially connected with Maya as we all guided him through this process. I had to ask myself whether he was thinking the role of Maya might best be played by Selena Gomez in his MFA production. Even an active female detective might still be seen onstage in very short skirts and enticing cleavage, although none had ever made an appearance like that in our case notes except for a few of Maya's Mata Hari efforts. I intentionally neglected to tell Rodrigo that Maya had been posing nude for me all through our first case. It seemed like that would add nothing to her onstage presence.

One of the things I've learned in this business is that reality has too many subsets to keep track of, and I was most interested to see what Rodrigo Ferrer's spin might be on ours, young as he was. It would be, I was certain, uniquely his own. We had never been fans of drama in life, since we usually spent most of our time fighting it off. Painting also demands a sense of calm and careful focus. I had never been a theater person, either, but I'd found myself in recent months warming to the opening night as it approached. After extracting his chosen case record from the files, Rodrigo Ferrer had come by the house twice more to record conversations with all three of us in an attempt to capture, as he said, "the tone and timbre of your speech for the way it would come across onstage." It did not escape me that he asked us to repeat actual phrases from the case record. We'd already given him permission to quote from it freely whenever it was helpful.

Tonight we were guests of honor for the opening night of *Identity Crisis*, the rather violent story of our eighth case. Before the lights were dimmed I turned and looked back over the audience. The show had sold out. It was not a large theater; it could've been about 125 seats. Cody leaned across me and said to both of us, "Break a leg, kids." I wondered if that was an omen. Of course, it was not another case at all, only fantasy and reenactment. Our last case had ended late in May in Guatemala, and this was early October. It was merely a pleasant theater evening with a uniquely personal twist, a welcome and stimulating break from our normal routine.

Or so we then thought.

CHAPTER TWO

Identity Crisis, in the play version, was structured in three acts with an intermission between the second and third. On the thrust stage, for the opening scene the entire set consisted of a single garbage can on the left side, and at the back, a five-panel door hung upright in a frame without a wall around it. There were also two straight-back chairs set on one side as if against a wall. Like any artist, I wanted to encourage the young playwright, but this struck me as minimal indeed. But then, I hadn't been to a play in fifteen years and I may not have been up to date on current theater trends. Like so many other things in the arts, they must be subject to the whims of fashion. Another possibility was that, as a master's thesis production, money for props and costumes would've been understandably minimal. I was sure that the actors were working without pay, or were only paid after all the other expenses were covered. Perhaps Rodrigo Ferrer would later become huge as a playwright and call everyone back at top Actors' Equity rates.

Still, it was clearly going to take an enormous reach of imagination for the audience to buy into our story, to participate in it and to live it (or in our case, to relive it). Our approach in investigation was the exact opposite—everything hung on the precise detail of the event. But wasn't the modern theater set often only a hook for the audience to hang their imagination on? Wasn't the fact that it compelled your participation from such sketchy elements both its weakness and its strength? This was, after all, our story; we were going to see ourselves onstage through the mind of not only the novice playwright, Rodrigo Ferrer, but of the director and all of the actors. This was a strange sensation I had never imagined before. This was not a major production in any way, but had we in the Paul Zacher Agency ever been so important before? Certainly there had never been an audience of this size to appraise our skills.

My case notes, the skeletal but factually exact narrative Ferrer had worked from, were never intended to furnish a basis for two hours of theater. Every shortcoming and inaccuracy that appeared in my interpretation of events as I'd written them up four years before had been passed on to him. I knew I had gotten better at it since then. When we'd given him permission to use what he could from our files I'd never thought the process through to this point, never imagined we'd be sitting there on opening night to view a painful chapter from our own lives. With no warning Maya's hand gripped my wrist.

"Paul! It's time now to stop worrying," she whispered hoarsely. "You're almost grinding your teeth. It'll be all right. Let them do their version of it."

A case of the jitters had clearly come over me, and I nodded without enthusiasm.

At that moment the lights dimmed. Slinking through the audience on the left side aisle, a nimble figure leaped into the shadows onstage. Struggling with a semi-secure fastening on the lid, he began grubbing about in the garbage can, throwing papers and bloody bandages to the floor of the stage. I recognized the scene, as I had imagined it in my notes. The location was the parking area of a cosmetic surgery clinic in the nearby city of Querétaro. The man was looking for needles he could reuse with the tiny bag of heroin in his pocket. And that's how it began, once again.

Like most of our real cases, the one we had called *Identity Crisis* had spawned its share of lowlife characters. Worst of all, it was a case where the three of us had barely survived with our lives, and then only due to luck. Despite its benign effect that time, luck is not a reliable survival skill in the detective business. If most professional Las Vegas gamblers give it no respect, it gets even less from us.

Because the cast had only nine members, I knew

that some had to be playing more than one role. That was a joke. How could anyone step into Cody's outsize frame and also play another person in the story? How much was going to be required of the audience to suspend their disbelief, as an actor went from one role to the other? Did they merely switch hats? (Although I recalled seeing this done a number of years ago, and it had worked at the time.) Who could play both Maya and another woman (or man, since I was not above suspecting the cast might possess this level of flexibility)?

Still, half an hour into the play and deeply engaged by the narrative, I found myself unable to stop smiling, even though Rodrigo Ferrer had written little humor into it. Maya was leaning forward with her elbows on her knees, her chin resting on her clasped hands, hanging on every word and completely absorbed. Cody grunted softly now and then as if to indicate they had gotten something right about him. This was one of the benefits of a front row seat. The casting had disappointed none of us, even if it was not predictable. In this sense, it echoed every real case we'd had.

For personal reasons, let me start with the character named 'Paul Zacher.' He might have been five-foot-eleven, and so an inch and a quarter shorter than I am in real life, but that was merely a quibble. He was elastic in his movements and occasionally funny, as I sometimes hope to be, so that was a good fit, or at least good writing from Ferrer. He had taped our conversational styles to good ends.

As he walked onstage, notebook in hand, the 'Cody Williams' character was initially a disappointment, since at six-foot-three, everyone who knew him always looked first at the real Cody's height, since his physical presence was so imposing. But this was an audience that did not know him, and what this actor gave us, barrel chested and formidable at about five-foot-nine, with big hands, feet, and shoulders, was the Cody presence with a lot of the right attitude. I looked around to see if Rodrigo Ferrer was in the audience—as he must've been on opening night—but I couldn't spot him in that light.

The actor who played 'Diego Delgado,' our long-time contact in the Judicial Police of San Miguel, was a Mexican, Ruben Gonzalez, and he looked too young for the role, but he was doing a convincing job otherwise. He had the properly grave air of small city Mexican officialdom, but with a hint of irony and an element of tentativeness that came from dealing with well-connected gringos throughout his career.

Maya's feelings about the actress who played her were more mixed, as if the honesty of a role depended on different things. "My butt is smaller than hers. I'm sure you noticed that."

I nodded gravely. "And that is true. If this were about butts more than it is, then you would have a legitimate question about casting. As you suggested before, this actress is not as young and compelling as you are. I think she might still convey the essence of your role in this story. As you have seen, many of her costumes are loose fitting. While none of her clothing is sprayed on like your jeans always are, I think her voice and tone are still quite like yours."

"Thank you. But now I think you've been looking more at Mercy Buchanan."

For purposes of the anonymity we'd required, Rodrigo Ferrer had called Mercy Buchanan's character simply Rebecca, with no last name. In the real files for this case, Mercy Buchanan had offered scant mercy to anyone around her. She also presented an interesting hurdle in this drama. The role was what is called the *ingénue*, the "naïve" young girl right off the bus from Dubuque, but in this case that was only skin-deep, since she was loaded with deadly intent. On the day we returned to our bed and breakfast room in Guanajuato during the real case, Mercy was waiting in our bed and had tried to pull a gun on us when she realized I wasn't alone. Maya, being prepared more than I was, shot her dead. We were both anticipating that coming scene when the intermission began, so we all got up to stretch and went outside with the crowd. If the rest of the audience did not know what was coming next, we did. So far Rodrigo Ferrer had been following the course of the case without any deviation.

I had observed Rebecca throughout the first part of the play, and for me, she lacked the degree of malicious seriousness that had been just under the skin of Mercy Buchanan. Her innocent look needed to be contradicted by something more subtly evil in her manner.

In the lobby Cody bought a fifty-peso ticket for a glass of red wine, and realizing that we needed to relax a bit, so did Maya and I. Under the portico outside on Avenida Independencia, the failing sun provided a filtered but flattering light to an excited audience. Little traffic passed us on the cobblestone street. Observation is my long suit, both as an artist and a detective, so I split off and wandered through the crowd, listening for comments. Being a painter is not a high profile job, so most people who weren't friends of ours did not know me by sight. They might recognize my paintings before they recognized me, and for the Agency, a degree of anonymity was usually an asset when we worked.

Maya and Cody always did well when left to themselves. He had been in love with her for years. That fact had long been out in the open and it was never a problem, but he relished his time alone with her. I was only three meters away when I heard the first snippet of the surrounding conversation. It was from a red-haired woman in a Day of the Dead print dress. She had an East Coast accent and a voice that carried.

"I met that Zacher guy once, you know, Elliot, the one that just walked by? I never told you that. It was when there was still that nightclub over by the Fabrica Aurora, la Cava I think it was called? I don't know where Maya Sanchez was that night, but there was a Colombian singer working onstage who was to die for, and Zacher was clearly dying for her. Like, I mean coming out of his chair to applaud her on every song."

I didn't turn to see Elliot's response. Unable to deny what she'd said, I picked up my pace a little. This had happened on our fourth case when Maya walked out on me for two months because she couldn't control all the risk we were taking on. She had sworn she would never come back. I paused again when I heard an emotional note from another couple.

"I just have a very bad feeling about this, Janis, OK? Didn't you notice that there are more women in this cast than men?"

"You think the victim will be a woman."

"Yes, I do. I don't like to see women murdered. It's not right."

"You're too sentimental, Dick. Women get murdered all the time, and anyway, it's only a play."

What did that mean? Had they seen the case files too?

"I just ordered one of those brass plaques to put beneath my doorbell," one woman said to another at the edge of the cobblestone street.

"What plaque is that?"

"It says Premises Protected by The Paul Zacher Agency."

"You're kidding. What on earth can they do?"

"Well, no one has tried to break in lately."

While I enjoyed this, I also knew the idea must have been some former client's joke. The other woman laughed too. A moment later the music came up on the outside speakers to signal our return for the start of the second half.

CHAPTER THREE

I turned back and took Maya's hand, and we all went inside. I didn't recognize the music, but while it was vaguely modern in feeling, it also carried a sense of tension and foreboding. Inside, the houselights were up but the stage was still dark. I could only make out a suggestion of a bed with a bold print fabric coverlet toward the back, and that same roving door in a frame, now located near the front at the left corner of the stage. From the contour of the linens, the bed looked occupied. In the tentative lighting, I couldn't make out any more detail, but I didn't have to. I'd had nightmares about this scene in the past, and so had Maya, even more than I had.

Knowing all too well what was coming, we sat down with an air of artificial calm, but instead of releasing it, Maya gripped my hand tighter. On my left, Cody's face displayed a grim look. He hadn't been present at this critical scene during the original case, but he had come upon it shortly after. Around us, the audience fell deadly silent, catching the same emotional cues. The mood of the music reflected the vague ghostly form on the bed.

When the music stopped, the room was so silent you could almost hear people blink. Nothing happened for about thirty seconds. Pace is everything in theater, I thought, and they very well know it here. Enter the 'Paul' and 'Maya' characters from the lobby, casually walking down the left aisle as if they had no care in the world, possibly after a glass of wine or two at lunch. I was struck to see they were also holding hands. How close was art going to imitate life in this piece?

Had Rodrigo Ferrer envisioned this drama as a tragedy, or only a disaster? It seemed like tragedy required a moral lesson of great force to give it the proper resonance, a statement that illuminated a basic fault in the human condition, one people could never quite escape. Looking back on the actual case, it had been no more than several bad characters who'd been killed in the process of committing their criminal acts and trying to kill us. Any cosmic resonance it might have had died with them.

I'm sure my face wore a grim look as Cody leaned toward my ear. "It's only theater," he said, trying to bluff a grin out of me. "Just try to see it that way as this part plays out."

I couldn't respond, realizing how much I didn't want to see this again. The house lights faded as the stage lights came up. As he and 'Maya' reached the freestanding door, 'Paul' searched his pocket for a room key and failed to come up with it. "Do you have it?" he said to her, his voice breaking the artificial silence.

To me, at that moment, he sounded more cheerful and naïve than I would've been; than in fact I really had been at that moment, although I'd had no idea of what was awaiting us inside that room. This actor hadn't been on as many cases as we had. His body language was already suggesting that even though he knew he wasn't at the heart of what came next, he was still slightly apprehensive. In contrast, the 'Maya' character was calm and focused as Maya herself had really been in that moment.

Instead of answering or reaching in her pocket, she first touched the door with two spread fingers on the lock edge, and under that slightest pressure, it opened inward inch by inch. This was a bit of business from the director, Ken Fairfax, and it carried all the tension of a noir film scene by Hitchcock. The tentative, anticipatory quality of her gesture was perfectly expressed. From somewhere above and behind us, the sound booth provided a subtle squeak of hinges. While it was not at all overdone, it was still enough to alert the dozing young woman on the bed. Beyond that, the audience was utterly silent. Yet in the filmy air hung something like a subtle buzz or white noise, a hovering atmospheric mist we were surrounded by as we waited to see what was going to happen next. Maybe it was only the hum of anticipation growing inside our heads.

The obscure figure on the bed suddenly bolted upright into the beam of a spotlight from the ceiling. It was 'Mercy Buchanan' (now called Rebecca because the author wasn't using real names), scrambling for what could only have been a gun somewhere under the sheets.

Yanking her own gun out of her purse, 'Maya' yelled, "Stop right there!" She fired a quick warning shot into the ceiling. In that intimate theater space the sound was deafening, wrenching people from their seats, even though it had to be a blank round, since no plaster dust or chips fell from above. When Rebecca ignored her, still clawing for the gun as if she had dozed off waiting for me to appear and lost track of it within the sheets, 'Maya' stepped forward and fired again, this time directly at the girl's head.

In that thunderous moment, the audience groaned in shocked unison as Rebecca was thrown back-ward and sagged against the pillows. The illusion shat-tered and the confrontation became real at the instant it was finished. The sheet, which she had held against herself before with one hand, now slipped to expose a bare breast. That could hardly be intentional, at least not in this way. But the truly fatal fact was the small round hole that had appeared in the right side of her head. It could not have been makeup. The second shot 'Maya' fired from her revolver must have been a live round. The three of us in the Agency all knew what we had seen because we'd encountered it too many times before. A sudden death by gunshot has its own unique quality, one I've never seen in the movies. Some of the audience must have been convinced for an instant that it was a stunning breakthrough in theatrical realism before they realized they had just witnessed a murder.

The real Cody leaped to his feet. 'Maya' and 'Paul' were about to rush forward toward the victim when he leaped through the open stage door toward the bed and elbowed them aside. He could've just gone around it. Sudden shouts came from backstage. A Mexican man wearing jeans and a striped shirt bounded through the filmy curtain at the back. He reached Rebecca almost at the same moment as Cody and bent toward her face, pulling the sheet up again to cover her breast.

A surge of unsettled mumbling erupted from the audience, followed at once by a growing babble of panic. Two men began shouting something I couldn't make out. Moving unsteadily like she was about to faint, the actor playing 'Maya' dropped the gun to the stage near her feet. Slipping up behind her, I bent over, inserted my pen under the trigger guard, and picked it up. As she moved closer to the dead girl she put her hands to the sides of her coiled hair and screamed. The audience, which had continued to murmur and fret, fell silent for a shocked moment, then started to chatter and moan again in earnest.

The real Maya joined us onstage, already on her cell to Cruz Roja, the ambulance company, and then to Diego Delgado. He was the prosecutor with investigator's duties from the Judicial Police we normally dealt with on all our cases. From Maya's look, he must not have been answering, off duty at that hour. I stood with the lethal revolver ridiculously rocking back and forth in the middle of the ballpoint pen in my left hand, wondering what to do next. Three other people had rushed through the curtain from the back. Ken Fairfax was one, and another was a young woman I didn't recognize. Was she the prop mistress? The stage lights and the house lights were suddenly all blazing at once. In the brilliant light, absurdly, the phrase *full disclosure* came into my head. The sound from the booth above and behind the audience, of course, had gone dead. Other actors appeared onstage. Among them I saw 'Cody,' and then, 'Diego Delgado.' Soon he would meet his real counterpart, just as we had ours.

The real Cody bent over Rebecca, the 'Mercy Buchanan' character, trying to assess the degree of her injury, but it didn't look good from where I stood. He was saying something in a low tone to the man in jeans. While Rebecca's eyes were still half open, no tone remained in her neck muscles as he moved her head slightly. Her open mouth was slack and expressionless. Watching from fifteen feet away, I could see that when Cody touched her shoulders and lifted her wrist she had the soft and floppy response of a rag doll. Shaking my head, I turned back toward the audience. This scene possessed far too much of the feel of the actual event in our eighth case. I had never for a moment forgotten the real incident this was based on, and if tonight the details were somewhat off, the essence of the original moment was perfectly framed.

Reality occasionally interrupts my dreams about the conflict between art and life. This was worse than anything I'd ever seen there.

Most of the audience was now standing. Those who weren't seemed close to fainting. Many arms were waving. Some people were pointing at the stage. Heated arguments were underway. I heard, "Oh my God!" a dozen times. A few women were weeping. The real Maya was pacing back and forth beside me on the edge of the stage. It was the kind of scene she hated more than any other, but she knew we'd never be able to avoid them. "Why her, why now?" she was saying more to herself than to me. I could only shake my head. Maya tried Delgado's cell number again and apparently reached him. She walked toward the far corner of stage front with the phone pressed to her ear.

A calmer couple from the back row stood up and marched purposefully down the aisle toward me. I stepped off the stage, still holding the smoking gun with my pen under the trigger guard and trying to keep the barrel from pointing at people as we waited for Delgado and the forensics crew. Knowing what was coming, I felt useless. The Agency had no authority there; our only role would be as three witnesses among too many.

"You're the real Paul Zacher, aren't you? Don't try to deny it." This was the woman from the couple that approached me.

"Doesn't seem like it now, although I've been accused of that before. Talk to me later when I've got some clues, other than this." I looked awkwardly back at the revolver in my hand.

"Even so," the man said, "I saw it happen. I want to be your first witness tonight, since I know I can help."

I turned and faced him. He was a forty-something man of medium height, with a pale complexion and blue eyes. He had thin hair and lips with a nervous manner, but even obviously agitated, his expression still seemed genuine. "Go ahead. Did you see something I missed from the front row?"

"Bill is a wonderful observer," the woman said. "He's a painter like you are."

I shook his hand without embracing him. Bill was also wearing a bow tie in México, which did not enhance his credibility, but in this business I have learned to be tolerant. "Being a painter always works for me. What did you see tonight, Bill?"

"At the back of the stage," he said slowly, turning to point and get it right, "on that far left edge of the backdrop, someone pulled the curtain aside no more than two inches, as if to see what was going to happen just before the second shot was fired. I mean it was right after the first one, so this happened in that tiny instant between them. Whoever it was must've known it had to be quick, and he was already in position. Naturally, everyone in the audience and onstage was looking at the woman scrambling around on the bed."

And as if to indicate that she was waiting for 'Paul' naked, as she was in the actual case, Rebecca had been holding the sheet over her chest with her right hand as she scrambled for the gun with her left.

"Before?" I said, leaning toward him. "You're sure you saw this *before* that second shot was fired?"

"Yes, absolutely, because that subtle movement distracted me from the woman on the bed. It was like going on at the edge of my vision, and then only an instant later the second shot was fired."

"Exactly what did you see of that person at the edge of the curtain? Was it someone you could identify? As a painter, think carefully of the visual detail here. As you suggested, you're now my first witness, and you may turn out later to be the best."

Bill stood up a centimeter taller. "Well, I'm not

totally sure of this, OK, Mr. Zacher?"

"Paul."

"But I wanted to talk to you first. I thought I saw a glimpse of bright red hair. Like unnaturally bright, even clown costume bright. That's all. Nothing of the face below, except that maybe it had kind of pale skin."

"Could you identify that face if you saw it again?"

He paused as if ashamed. "No. I wish I could be more helpful, but I really don't think I could. But there was also this; it was not at head height, but much closer to the floor, as if someone was sneaking in on his hands and knees, hunkering down. You know how stealth always draws your eye?"

And it always did. "So if he was creeping along, his face would've been angled downward somewhat," I said, nodding. To me, admitting his uncertainty gave Bill more credibility. Some witnesses like to maintain their position at the center of a case by promising more than they can deliver, and they'll improvise detail to do it.

"Bill shows at a real art gallery here in town," the woman said, with a determined lift of her eyebrows, "just like you do, only it's not the same one." She managed an encouraging smile.

"You've been very helpful indeed. This tells me that someone backstage knew what was coming next, but even more, that person wanted to witness Rebecca's death first hand. If you have a pen and a piece of paper, could you write down your contact info for me? We're just getting started here, and my pen is tied up at the moment, since I don't want to touch this gun. I'll have to get back to you as this develops."

"Sure." Staring at the gun barrel, which was no longer smoking, he pulled out his business card, scrawled something on the back of it and handed it to me. "I can still smell that gun, by the way."

"So can I. Thank you very much, Bill..." I looked at the card. "Cramer."

As I walked back onstage Cody was coming toward the front, frustration gathering around his head like a thundercloud. He threw his hands in the air, waving them. "She's gone, totally gone. I'm sure she didn't even feel it. I hope she didn't, poor kid. Christ, I think I've seen way too much of this for a single lifetime. And at her age, really."

Maya went over to hug him. Her instincts were always right on.

'Maya' and 'Paul' were now gone from the stage too, in their own way, and somewhere backstage another person was shouting, this time in Spanish. I could understand the cast people scattering. In the world of simulated emotion, why stay around to display your very real grief? Or guilt? We could leave most of this to Delgado. Like Bill Cramer, my volunteer witness, we would offer our testimony and step back into the crowd to let the official version prevail.

As it usually did in this town, as in most others.

Like interference in a large speaker, a high-pitched screech tore through the sound system all over the theater. People groaned as they grabbed at covering their ears. Had someone bumped the amplifier? If it was only accidental, it was still the proper note for that moment in a play that had tragically spilled over into the audience.

CHAPTER FOUR

Fifteen minutes passed before four cops in black field uniforms, black helmets, and bulletproof vests surged through the lobby and down the two side aisles toward the stage. Were they expecting a riot? At their appearance the crowd grew subdued. In front of this distraught assembly, Licenciado Diego Delgado followed with a measured but authoritative step, as if he had these cops on a leash. He was wearing his normal brown suit, this time with the jacket opened to the gun on his hip. From our long experience with him, any of us in the Agency could've written his next lines.

The storm troopers swept the stage clear toward the back, except for the body on the bed. I stepped into the aisle and looked back to see that more police had sealed the two lobby entrances. This was good procedure, if a little late. There was no way to know who had slipped away in the midst of the shock wave that immediately followed the shooting. I also wondered whether there was an exit backstage. Esquivel, the forensics man, and his assistant arrived a minute later. He was drawing on his gloves as he came through the lobby entrance. I met him at the bottom of the right side aisle and showed him the gun on the end of my pen, telling him how I'd picked it up just as 'Maya' dropped it on the stage, and I had made sure that no one else touched it.

Handling it gingerly, he broke open the .38 caliber revolver and looked into the cylinder. It contained three brass shells in adjacent chambers, and only two had been fired. The first round in the sequence had not. He shook them out into his palm one at a time. That intact first shell was a blank. It had the characteristic crimping of the forward edges, which had never gripped a lead slug, but were only turned inward to retain the charge, detonated for its noise. He slid it back into the cylinder. The second shell had the same crimping, but it had been fired, forcing the crumpled edges outward from the detonation, but unevenly, so they were not fully smooth. This had to be the shell fired first onstage, into the ceiling, as a warning from 'Maya.' We would find no impact mark up there among the lights.

The last had been a normally loaded cartridge casing, also fired, smooth on the sides, and empty of the slug it once held. This was the bullet that had killed Rebecca. I thanked Esquivel and moved away. This detailed demonstration was more than he would normally have given me at that stage of a case and without consulting his boss, Delgado, but I had preserved the gun for him exactly as it was when fired, and he knew that was worth a great deal in this crowd.

I knew that the arrangement of three spent and unfired cartridges in the cylinder was not right but at that moment I didn't want to try to sort out what it meant.

There might have been 145 people in the theater that evening, including the cast and crew. If I hadn't gotten to it first, anyone could've picked up the gun and started passing it around as a trophy. An individual crime scene witness will almost always act more intelligently than a crowd of them.

Meanwhile Esquivel's assistant had begun fingerprinting everyone who had been onstage or backstage, starting with Alfonso, the stage manager, who was now looking understandably overwhelmed. He stood three meters away with his back to the victim; most Mexicans prefer to have no contact with a fresh corpse, even if the shriveled bodies of saints dead for centuries are no problem.

The ambulance crew came in with no sense of urgency and briefly conferred with Delgado, then stepped to the edge of the stage for a moment. Paco Mora, the part time coroner, entered with his assistant trailing a stretcher on wheels. It was no secret that Mora spent most of the hours in his medical practice performing affordable plastic surgery on tourists. Being the coroner didn't offer enough employment to keep him busy, even though he also consulted with one of the funeral parlors on making their clients presentable for a long stint in eternity. I had always hoped he used different instruments for these procedures, and I am almost certain that he does.

I went back to my seat, waiting for the next move from Delgado. After he announced in Spanish that no one would be leaving the theater until released, most of the audience sat down again as well. But for the very real tragedy of the young actress who died, this could almost have been part of the play, *Identity Crisis*. Still, it had more elaborate costumes and too many extras in nonspeaking parts. They were busily prancing about in a series of moves that even as they labored to evoke authority, still lacked the properly coordinated choreography. Cody sat down next to me shaking his head. Maya gripped my hand.

The long hour that followed was a lesson in local police procedure, one we didn't need. Repeatedly my mind wandered back to the dead girl, Rebecca. She could never have imagined an ending like this. However this case developed for Delgado, I resolved to find out more about the victim on my own and try to bring her some justice.

As the physical evidence was being gathered, two plainclothes assistants of Delgado's took everyone's name and contact information. They checked this against their

IDs and asked them what they had seen before allowing them to leave. Anything else the Paul Zacher Agency might have done would've only interfered in this phase of the case, so we did what everyone else was doing and left without comment when we were released. This happened for us earlier than for many other audience members because we were seated in the front row. What followed was a grim and nearly silent drive back to the house on Quebrada where Maya and I tried to live a calmer life than this.

"How much I miss the resolution of that investigation," I said. "The one we would've seen onstage. Now it feels like we're thrust right back inside it."

We'd been given a great case of wine to celebrate a recent Agency outing, the one we'd filed as *Noble Rot*, but for this impromptu meeting in our loggia at the edge of the rear garden, we brought out a bottle of our usual Chilean working class red. There would be nothing to celebrate for a while for anyone involved at the San Miguel Play House. I could imagine as well the condition of the drama graduate student Rodrigo Ferrer, whose MFA playwright effort had been shattered by someone with a more pressing agenda. I wondered whether it was a person from his college, possibly a rival in the theater department? Yet, as I had heard from comments in the lobby going in after the break, Rebecca had been staying in San Miguel, was not connected with Ferrer's college, and was a part time resident from somewhere in New England, a long haul from México.

By now we had settled in, and the dusky evening was fading into darkness. At the long plank table this period of twilight had often led to better insights. Perhaps it was because what seemed obvious was less so in that light, and nuance could be appreciated more clearly in indirect light.

"This murder of 'Mercy Buchanan,' or as they called her tonight, Rebecca, was in the truest sense an act of theater," Cody began while I pulled out the cork. I knew he'd been thinking this through on the way over.

"That goes without saying," I said. I hadn't been able to get the dead girl's image out of my mind.

Maya poured the wine as I lit the candles on the table and turned on the ground lights scattered throughout the foliage. In the deepening silence around us, it made for an eerie mood after what we'd seen. Since we'd come off duty, all of us needed some time to recover from witnessing a murder.

"But I mean literally," Cody continued, shaking his head with a touch of impatience. "Some killings are acts of stealth. They are either done purely as a murder, where the sole object is the death of another person, or where death is a side effect, intended or not, but not the main goal, as in a robbery or a home invasion where you encounter the owner or his neighbor. So when it requires an audience, as we saw tonight, there can be only one reason for that; it's to convey a message to the witnesses. It might be to humiliate the victim, or to degrade his position or authority, or hers, in this case."

"I know what you're thinking now, by starting with *his*," Maya said, leaning back into her wicker chair and folding her arms. "John Kennedy. You're going to talk about that day again."

"Exactly. Well, I'm the only one here who remembers it. I was only a kid at the time, although I've thought about it much more since. He was shot down in front of a crowd of thousands of his admirers. It was a public execution, just as hangings used to be in the old days. The people who wanted him dead also wanted to deliver a message. It was a *demonstration* of their power, even though they had set Oswald up as their official patsy."

"Well, then we can start with the idea that it was not the 'Maya' character tonight who wanted to kill Rebecca," I said. "That was only too obvious. We do like to look behind what we're handed on the opening move when it's such a clear set up."

"Thank you for that," Maya said. "You're saying the 'Maya' character was only a pawn in this. As they call it in chess, it's a gambit. Is that the word?"

"Regrettably, that's almost my first response," I said. "I could be proven wrong as it develops."

"But I think it must have been more about punishing the actress who played me, since she was set up to pull the trigger. Let's call her by her real name now. I got it from the playbill. It's Simone Garfield. I don't want my name mixed up with this MFA project anymore, OK? Rodrigo was an earnest guy, but I'm out of it now. I already killed that girl once in real life and I have to live with that all the time. I don't need it pushed in my face again when I'm out trying to have a good time."

"Didn't we know it wasn't going to be altogether a good time?" I said. "*Identity Crisis* was one of our nastiest cases, and one where each of us barely survived, and then only from luck." The truth was that in this business, if you only survive because of luck, then you're running on empty.

This was followed by a moment of awkward silence as we all recalled how it had really gone.

"I didn't try to do it," said Cody, shaking his head. "I heard Simone say that to Delgado when he first came onstage. It's the prototype alibi, starting at age three. I'm sure Eve also used it for the first time after eating that apple. She must've invented it as she stood there talking to Adam, holding the core behind her back."

"If," I said, nodding, "this is really about punishing Simone Garfield, setting her up to take the rap for this murder, then poor Rebecca really was no more than a sacrificial victim, and her death was only collateral damage. She was the innocent ingénue in this drama that she also probably was in life. To me it was really cold to kill her off like that, I mean *really* cold, and to hang her murder on someone who had no intention of doing it. In my view, we are dealing here with a person who is deeply evil. Nothing less than that."

"I know you never like to believe that," said Cody, quietly, and with an ironic look that reflected long experience. "You usually like to go for the shades of gray scenario, the unintended consequences set up by a person in a tough spot who commits a crime to escape it. But he's not always a bad guy to start with, am I right?"

"Time and time again that's been my observation," I said. "And most of our cases bear that out. But you've been in this business much longer than I have."

"Then what is this killer thinking?" said Maya, jumping in before Cody could respond. "Was he trying to punish me, as the real Maya? Was he somehow connected to the original case and we overlooked him? Because Delgado made no move to arrest Simone Garfield for the murder, although he still could later. Often he takes the simplest answer as the truth, but this shooting did not fool him either."

"That's an interesting idea, that this killing could be part of our original case," I said, trying to imagine this, four years later, but I still couldn't quite believe it.

"Yet," Cody said, "look at this. The victim was

an American girl, I understand, a college student taking a break. She'd done some summer theater before, although not much, but she was also known to the playwright, in what way, I don't know. Rodrigo Ferrer told us he was doing the casting, with some help from Ken Fairfax, the theater manager. Casting was part of his thesis, even if directing wasn't. If Delgado starts to get some heat from the mayor's office and feels he has to make an arrest, Simone would be the obvious candidate. She's not out of the woods yet."

"Maybe Simone would be the sacrificial victim for Delgado to lock up to take the pressure off his office while he thinks harder about who the real killer is," Maya said. "Since it's the death of another gringo, he's going to end up between the sword and the wall again."

"Is that cynical too, for Delgado, to bust her, Simone Garfield, I mean?" I said.

"Maybe," she said, "but we've always taken our share of outside pressure too. We all know how it is. It can build up when you're expected to solve a case within a certain time. That you can hardly ever do. Most of our cases have been like a bullfight. Each one has its own rhythm and it has to be played out in its own way."

"And it's not always the bull that dies," Cody said, with a degree of satisfaction. Among the three of us, he was clearly the bull, so there may have been a self-serving element to that comment.

I studied Maya's face for a moment. This was one of her cultural insights that was right on. Of the three of us, Maya had always been the most sensitive to both risk and outside pressure. No one could blame her. We all had our ways of coping. Sometimes Maya and I drank too much cognac at the end of the day. Sometimes Cody watched too much football. I had always wondered whether the multimillion-dollar choreographed violence of the NFL somehow offset for him the irrational low rent mayhem we often encountered in our cases. On the easily contained television screen it was more like a nearly abstract repetitive ritual, with well-defined break points to catch your breath. In the Agency we'd never had those. Most cases could go from bleak boredom to raging panic in a heartbeat.

"The main question that comes up for me," Cody said, swirling his wineglass in the flickering light from the table candles, "is how the number of rounds in the murder gun was altered. I would think that if Simone, as she was playing 'Maya,' was planning to fire one shell at the ceiling as a warning and the other at Rebecca when she ignored it, then a third bullet, the only live round in the gun, had to be added before she put it in her purse. The script called for her to fire the gun twice, and then the live bullet was added at the third position of the three shells, so the firing pin was reset to rest on the first chamber, loaded with a blank. It would then be advanced as the trigger was pulled to fire the second round, also a blank, for the first shot. That's the one that went into the ceiling, because when you fire a revolver, the cylinder automatically advances to the next round, not the one the firing pin was resting on as you started to pull the trigger. I'm going to assume Simone Garfield had her stage purse with her, but we'll have to verify that. Maybe it was only just handed to her in the lobby as she walked into the scene. I don't know how that works in the theater."

"But obviously, someone else did know. You sound like we have a case going already," I said. As head of the Zacher Agency, this was always Maya's call. Determining which cases we took was her way of controlling our risk. That was effective less often than she liked.

"I am having mixed feelings about taking on this case," she said slowly. "But we are already involved since we were witnesses placed in the best seats in the house. And what is more, isn't this play about us? How could we be less involved? If it's an effort to frame Simone Garfield, isn't it also a slap in the face for us? I think there is a message in this, just as you were saying, Cody."

"What is it?" I said.

"It's that now you *have* to solve this case, you pretentious self-important small town detectives. Let's see if you're really as good as you think you are."

That stopped the conversation for a moment. "I wonder if that's getting too personal?" I said. We were starting to get into some of the detail of why I might think that when my phone went off. It was Ken Fairfax, the director of the theater and of the play.

"I think I can imagine what you're all talking about right now," he said. "I wish I could be there, but I'm not finished here, and I won't be for a while. Delgado and his crew haven't left yet. I just can't believe this happened to Rebecca. I feel completely responsible, although I don't know how I could've prevented it."

"I'm very sorry that happened tonight. It's nothing but a tragedy for you and even more for that young girl. What's happening now where you are?"

"Continuing questioning of the cast and company. Inspector Delgado is locked in the dressing room with the prop mistress now."

"He's a *licenciado*."

"Whatever. I haven't talked to either of the other investors, but I'm going to make a command decision right now. I want the Paul Zacher Agency to investigate this case. No one could ever get closer to it than you people are already. I'll give you carte blanche starting tomorrow to talk to everyone here. When I get home, if I ever do tonight, I'll email you the contact info for everyone that was in the production in any capacity whatsoever."

"Thanks, Ken. I appreciate that, but are you saying you don't trust Diego Delgado to handle this on his own?"

"How can I tell? You've worked with him before, and all I know about that is from Rodrigo's research in your files. But I still saw his manner as he questioned Simone tonight and now I'm worried. I don't want to see her framed for this. She's a good person as well as an excellent actor, and I've known her for years. I gave Simone her first part."

"OK, I'll make a command decision too, even though I'm not the head of the Agency anymore." Maya and Cody had both picked up on what he was saying and were nodding briskly. "We'll take the case starting tonight."

"Great! Who do you want to begin with?"

"Tomorrow I'd like to begin with you, Ken, mainly for an overview. With so many things going on I need to place it all in context. Shall we say at ten o'clock at the theater? As usual I'll be front row center, since I suspect that the next act of this drama is only beginning. I also wouldn't mind catching a few of the rehearsals for your next production when they start. I expect to find a lot of improvisation there, and that's always my favorite part, since I've seen so much of it in other cases."

In my experience, improvisation, while a wonderful training tool for actors and playwrights, can easily turn into that patch of quicksand where criminals soon find themselves out of their depth. Unlike truth, where you only have to remember the facts, lying requires you to recall what you made up, which is often much harder to do.

But any talk of the next production was rash, given what had fallen into our laps.

CHAPTER FIVE

The following morning looked bright and polished as I pulled up at the San Miguel Play House on Calle Independencia. The street appeared to have been scrubbed clean by the explosive events of the night before. But I knew that was not quite true. It had also been both obscured and veiled by airborne debris. I expected more of that inside. I already knew that front and center was not the seat the suspects would prefer for me. Illusions play best when directed at the fourth row back or more, where the detail is not quite so clear. Depending on the lighting, the finger movements can blur. Thinking of the stage purse that held the gun, I could easily see that it was big enough to conceal the hand that added the live bullet to the cylinder.

Ken Fairfax was waiting at the door, giving orders to a man in coveralls for hanging a new set of lights, now scattered on the lobby floor. His level of absorption in this merely mechanical task underlined his need for distraction. It was too bad I was not there to provide any.

I had first met him two or three years before in a context I could not now recall, perhaps at a party or a charity benefit, but I thought of him as a fixture of the cultural life of San Miguel. I knew he had made the rounds of some of the key jobs in his field, as a director, producer, and a longtime actor. As he faced me now, it was easy to see him as a slightly faded leading man type. Still forthright and demonstrative in his mid fifties, his movements may have become more studied, but his grasp of those roles was probably more profound, more insightful. I wasn't sure the intense black color of his hair convinced me, but I was much closer to him than I would've been sitting in the audience.

"Well, this is just the worst nightmare of my career," he said immediately. "It's beyond tragedy. You can start with the brutal death of Rebecca, who was caught in a crossfire we do not understand, and now one of my other two investors is pulling out, if you can imagine that. Fortunately he's not the larger of the two, only the more skittish one. 'I can't take this kind of heat anymore,' he said to me last night after I talked to you. As if it was on him! He has no idea how I feel today."

"But I do, Ken, and I'm very sorry to hear that. Still, people in the States are often nervous about México. The press and the government are both whipping it up all the time. I can tell you, though, that those attitudes have nothing to do with this crime."

"Thank you. I hope you Zacher Agency people can do something about this, because now I'm afraid where that Delgado person intends to go with it."

"I understand, but we've dealt with him on many cases before this one, and he's never been unreasonable." Mostly, I thought, or only occasionally impossible. But why get into naked probabilities so early in a case?

"So, where should we start today?" Fairfax said, brightening only a little.

"That's easy. Call it stage politics. That will often mask a deeper emotional current. Something nasty is going on here."

Ken frowned and nodded slowly. "Paul, have you had any theater experience?"

"No, my only experience is in painting and in life. I know that's not the best preparation for something like this."

"OK, but they make a good starting point, if somewhat incomplete in range. Take the life part and triple the range."

"All right, so now at least I'm getting a sense of the scale here."

"Theater is the amplifier of life. It puts our existence on a stage and gives it a larger voice. If you think of the great amphitheaters of ancient Greece, then we are getting somewhere. We can proceed with good expectations." He reached over and grasped my hand in a belated handshake. "There are a lot of reasons to be an actor, and not all of them begin with ego. Most, however, end with ego."

"Of course," I said. "We all come to a bad end, but which of them end in murder?"

"Many of them do. The better question for now is whether it's in the play or not."

"I do like it that you have a serious overview. I'll be surprised if many of the actors do. Their job must be far more focused and specific."

"As it has to be," Ken said. "If you're directing, as I was with this piece and a lot of others, then you are the resident god presiding over the birth of an expanding universe. Your task is to breathe life into it in the areas where it's faint or struggling. Directing is like being a midwife on a grand scale. Sometimes you have to slap it on the butt to bring out its true voice. At other times you have to rein it in."

"Reality doesn't matter."

"It does at the box office, but only then and when you write the paychecks and pay the bills later. Please understand here, Paul, that even in this situation, reality is a marginal consideration. It never circumscribes what you can do onstage."

"I've often felt that myself, but perhaps for different reasons, and I do enjoy being able to dismiss it when I want to. In painting, reality doesn't go far enough. Still, we have to come up with some semblance of reality to make sense of this. Rebecca died for real reasons. To deny that reality is to insult her. Frankly Ken, to give her some respect by finding out why and how she died is why I'm here. It's why the Agency signed on."

"I thought you were here because we hired you."

I grinned at this. We are very far from always being financially motivated. "So yes, you hired us, but that only works when our motives overlap with the client's. We've done plenty of pro bono cases."

"All right. Let's look at the hard reality. Where do you want to start?"

"Backstage."

Fairfax nodded. He said a few words to the man working on the lights, locked the lobby doors behind us, and we went inside.

During the performance the three of us in the Agency had naturally been focused on the stage, and then on the audience once the murder had taken place. But while the reasons for Rebecca's death may have been deeply buried, the physical setup for the crime had happened in the confined area behind the back curtain. That, I felt, was where we would find the *how*. The *why* could be sorted out with more interviews.

Ken Fairfax and I crossed the empty dimly lit stage, passing through a gauzy backdrop into a grayish half-light. There were no windows. It was a veiled space where illusions could easily be assembled and pushed out toward the audience. Little was offered for serious lighting. What was the need? No one wished to call attention to what went on back there. That was all the better, in this case, I thought. We stepped off the rear part of the stage to the same floor level as at its front. Although the stage had continued for some distance behind the sheer curtain, the area below and behind that was shallow. Here in the center was the square wooden table where the props were held in readiness, now bare. I put my hands on my hips and looked around.

Against the outer walls on both sides were enclosed aisles where the actors could enter from the lobby unseen by the audience. On the left offstage a short run of six steps led up to a small platform that could be, for example, the balcony in *Romeo and Juliet*, or the podium in *Julius Caesar*. Behind that, a few more steps went up to a place I couldn't make out that well in the dim light.

"What's up there?" I said to Ken, pointing into the gloom. He motioned me to follow him. Passing the door hung in a frame without a wall that had served so many entrances and exits in *Identity Crisis*, I stumbled on the horizontal bars at the floor that held it upright.

On that upper level we paused.

Ken pointed to the right. "Here's the women's restroom, and on the left of it is an exit." Behind us was that small balcony a few steps down.

The exit caught my eye. Ken located a square-headed key on his ring and we went out into a small dreary patio at street level. It offered three large dead potted palms and no furniture or sun umbrellas. A barred steel gate gave access to the street in front. Alarms were going off in my head. This case was now going to be more about who had access to the props and the means of entry or escape.

"Tell me about how admittance to this area is controlled."

Ken nodded. "Sure. The street gate is always locked. The women's restroom is open to the public before the curtain is raised–that's a metaphor since we have no front curtain at all on a thrust stage. It's open again during the break, and after the play finishes. This patio exit door is unlocked when the lobby opens an hour before show time. It's closed after we lock the front doors at the end of the evening. That's just the *bomberos* regulation for any public theater in San Miguel." The *bomberos* operated the fire department.

"That makes sense, of course, but doesn't that open the door, so to speak, for unauthorized access?"

Ken shrugged at this. "In theory, you could say that. But this backstage area is a relatively small space so full of people before and during a performance that it would be hard to come in unnoticed. The stage manager always has his eye on what's going on. He would spot you and call you out in a heartbeat. That's part of his job."

"So he would be overseeing literally all the traffic."

"Right."

What if there was a distraction of some kind? I thought. Someone could come in and add a live round to the gun if he had some inside help. We came back inside. At the bottom of the stairs a left turn led down to a few more steps, less than a full story below the main level.

"This," Ken said, "is what we call the dungeon." He motioned me toward the stairs and threw a light switch on the wall.

I nodded. "Of course. This is where you keep the bad actors."

He chuckled. "Actually we need them more on-stage." We walked down five steps into a cramped storage area. Everything was laid out on shelves along one wall. It was all paint cans, brushes, and tools, but the ceiling lights were a bit brighter there, focused mainly over a small workbench with a vice bolted to the front edge and a long row of screw drivers, nippers, pliers, and files along the back. Along the far edge two wood saws hung in slots in the counter top. In the center of the long wall was what I most wanted to see: an oak cabinet with a strong hasp and a stout padlock.

"Yes," Ken said, with a smile, sensing my logic. "Its reassuring to see that you're smarter than the actor who played you. This is the prop cabinet."

I tried to recall who that was; his name was Lance perhaps? The padlock was an American made Master. "Who has the keys to this?"

Ken Fairfax was already nodding. "Nicole the prop mistress, and of course, the stage manager, but Nicole has keys to most things in the building. I have a key too, as well as to every other lock in this building."

"No one else? I'd like to look inside it."

"That's all. You can understand why props are critical, even if they're not weapons. If you need one for the business onstage, it better be there when you go on." Fairfax pulled a key ring out of his jacket pocket and flipped through it. Many of them were labeled with a small paper tab. A few were enclosed with a colored ring. The lock opened easily and he pulled it off the hasp at the edge of the cabinet door.

Inside, the three shelves held a variety of odds and ends. I saw a carving knife with a blade that ended in a broad pad that could be fastened under a shirt next to the skin. There was a police whistle on a chain, and three cigars that this close didn't look real, although they appeared to have some ash at the end. Some other things I didn't pause to look through, since on the top shelf my attention was drawn by a squat cylindrical box labeled *Maxxtech 9 mm blanks 50 rounds*. I had never been a gun aficionado, but I often carried one and I usually knew what I was looking at.

"Delgado didn't take this box away to look at downtown?" I said.

"He only took one of the cartridges to compare with the fired blank round in the gun."

On the bottom shelf were three identical revolvers in a row pointing toward the back wall, and a leather shoulder holster. Ken stepped back as I pulled one out. "Don't worry, I'm comfortable with guns," I said.

"I'm not. Last week I was. Things change."

Setting the gun back down I paused and looked into his eyes. "Yes they do. You must be a wreck with all this."

"Of course I'm devastated about poor Rebecca. So very young, and I can't think of any reason she would be killed. Imagine her parents now. What are they going through? But it's not only about me and her family. This is like a stone dropped into a pool. The ring of unintended effects continues to expand outward, growing in size every day. My insurance agent is ready to kill himself."

"But this is México, Ken. In this culture doesn't that mean Rebecca was fated to be killed? By saying that I'm not treating her death lightly, but I mean, even under the law here, where's your liability for this? México is not like the U.S. People don't go about hanging responsibility on everyone around them."

"Delgado's not so sure. A lot of this depends on

his mood and how he reads it, and what charges he's going to file. That's mainly why I hired your agency. The insurance company is splitting the cost with me."

"I see." This was not great news. To a large degree we would now be dealing with gringos and their issues with México, which had long been impregnated with fear from the media. "So if I can find the real killer, the heat is off you and your insurer."

"Exactly, and I'm glad you get that so easily, although I'll never stop flogging myself over Rebecca's death. I know how crass the insurance thing must sound to you, but after the awful event of this murder, then much of what follows is only business with cold people in offices far away to the north. While that's the way it is, this must still be one of your dirtiest cases. I just can't believe it came from us, here at the theater. We think of ourselves as cultivated, sophisticated, and a cultural beacon in San Miguel." He threw his arms into the air. "Not safe, exactly, because we're always taking risks in our productions, but at least not ever dangerous in this way."

"Well, none of us can do anything about that now. We'll get to the bottom of this, and hopefully that will settle the real blame somewhere away from you and the theater group." Thinking of the actual *Identity Crisis* case of several years ago, I made a random gesture that I still somehow hoped he would read as sympathetic. Even though it was at the core of the drama, I was certain our original case couldn't help us now. It had come up again as no more than a framing device, a useful springboard to a master's degree in theater arts. What was going to happen to poor Rodrigo Ferrer over this? His thesis project would probably be reset to zero.

From the prop cabinet I pulled out each of the remaining three guns. Delgado had taken away the fourth; the murder weapon I recovered from the stage as it was dropped by 'Maya,' and saved it untouched for Esquivel. The cylinders of the guns remaining in the cabinet were all empty of any rounds. I put the barrel of each one to my nose. They all smelled cold and clean and recently oiled. Guns always have to be maintained, but I still wondered why they were waiting for me in that condition. On any case we like to ask a lot of questions, but not all of them matter. It's easy to get ahead of yourself there too.

I don't often like clean and perfect and innocent evidence; it raises a red flag, it points too clearly in one direction or another, but at the point in the case where we were, I could only move on. Only one shot and one gun had killed Rebecca Carson.

"The prop mistress would've made the choice of which of these guns was loaded with blanks and handed to 'Maya', isn't that right?" I said.

"Exactly. That would've been earlier on the day

of the opening, as the actors arrived. Then it would've been locked back into this cabinet until she showed it to Rebecca alone for her personal inspection before the play began."

"Is that always the theater custom?" I said.

"Yes, anyone the gun is going to be pointed at inspects it to see that it's either not loaded at all, or if is has cartridges, they're all blanks. That's also a mandate from the insurance company. They're understandably nervous about having guns onstage, and they like to share blame whenever they can."

"But it still looks mostly like common sense to me," I said.

"Absolutely."

Nothing else in the prop cabinet or in the room caught my eye. "What's next?" I said, snapping the lock back on the door myself to test its function.

"The wardrobe and dressing room. That's on the other side. Follow me."

We climbed back up the half staircase, passed behind the darkened rear portion of the stage and the empty prop table, and descended the same number of steps into a room larger and better lit than the dungeon.

"This is where the cast runs between appearances to change," I said.

"Exactly."

"But there are no props kept here, right?"

"Never, since the actors will always get their props after their costume change, unless it's something that's part of the change, like that dagger on a pad you noticed in the cabinet. You saw the prop table again as we passed."

So here, I thought, was an opportunity to add a live round to the murder weapon. According to what I'd just been told, Rebecca would've already inspected the revolver that killed her before she went on in the first act.

This began to look like a case that hinged on timing, to a degree we had rarely seen before. But doesn't the action of any play hinge on precise timing just as much? The actors would all be used to it. Wouldn't adding a bullet to a revolver cylinder in ten seconds be no problem? The person who did it would've considered it no more than a rehearsal, a routine deeply familiar to all of them. We paused at the bottom of the dressing room steps.

"So, what I see here is one big room without screens or alcoves. You've got a couple of makeup tables with chairs, with a wall of floor-to-ceiling wardrobe closets opposite. Does everybody change together? I can tell you that whenever I paint a nude model I give her a chance to change privately. That's basic art studio etiquette. "

"Well, yes, I'm sure, but we are always limited by the physical space, and the cast is usually small. Perhaps this looks a little awkward to you as a non-theater person, but it's the same in a lot of small theaters all over the States, and here in México as well. The story is one of imperfect resources."

"How about modesty? Doesn't that play a role too?"

"Fine, and when it does, that's imperfect too, but you're dealing in the art studio with only one actor and one costume change at a time, with no schedule, no duress. Here, when I'm changing I turn my back to the other people if it's more than just me. If they're more sensitive than that, some of the women will change in their restroom; but that requires a few additional steps away from the stage when timing matters. They also can't hear the stage manager from there, because he's never yelling. Often they don't bother to leave this room. It depends on what the change involves and who else is present. Some people, I will tell you, are so used to it that it just doesn't matter to them. It's an odd kind of intimacy here, almost like being in the trenches in wartime."

"Still, in looking for a motive, I'm tempted to see this as a place where budding relationships could grow. People can flirt. The actors are all here in their skivvies or less. Don't you think?"

Ken nodded with an air of slightly injured patience. "I wonder if you might be putting it rather crudely. As if they had any time to flirt as they listened for their next cue. It's calm now, but think of this room as a place where a dozen things are going on all at once. The stage manager is out there at the top of the steps studying the second hand on his watch. What you're imagining as a group of horny young people playing slap and tickle or grab ass in the dressing room is usually no more than two or three middle-aged or older actors trying to get into costume as fast as they can. It's more about Velcro than garters and lace. This is not Radio City Music Hall by any means. We've got no Rockettes here, thank God."

I tried to think of Rebecca in this context, but the Rockettes probably had to be eight inches taller to qualify.

"You're saying it's not like a mixed gender locker room during half time. But still, when Rebecca fell back her right breast was exposed. What was that costume about?"

"She was topless under that sheet, but she was wearing bike shorts below. The idea was that she would be tossing about enough to expose her bare arms and shoulders. It was going to be a variable amount of skin as she woke up and reached for her gun. It was a bit of a tease, nothing more than that, and that's common in a production like this. She didn't have a problem with it because she thought she could control her degree of exposure."

I thought for a moment. "Was there a seductive

side to Rebecca's character? Was she a tease?"

Ken scratched his neck as he thought about this. "Offstage? I think she was pretty normal for a young woman her age. But here it was onstage, after all, and she was the focus of attention in that scene. In that context she was willing to give the audience a little skin, but within limits that she defined for herself. I let her decide that based on her comfort level. When it comes to skin that's always my policy."

"Does it often come down to skin?"

"It's theater, and theater is about display, whether of emotions, skin or soul."

"Sure. Yet in dying she was overexposed."

"Now you're starting to get it, but that wasn't in the book or in her mind."

"I'm sure it wasn't, but you didn't hire me to discover that Rebecca was killed by poison in her teacup between the acts. We already know the means, so let's get real about some possible motives here."

"Yes, Rebecca Carson. Who would want her dead?" I heard a plaintive sigh in his voice. "God knows I didn't."

"Now you're playing Paul Zacher without the paintbrush."

Ken laughed, not without an element of bitterness. "I am, and I almost took that role for myself, but I'm too old by sixteen years. For me, casting ten years off either way is my limit. Rodrigo told me you were forty. Still, with my experience I think I would've done better than Lance did with that role. I'm sure you'll talk to him, but I thought he had a degree or so of holding back with it. Anyway, Rodrigo did the casting."

"He's high on our interview list, somewhere after Simone Garfield."

We took some time to look at the costumes. There weren't many. One was a generic police uniform. No argument about usefulness there. Next were a couple of men's sport coats. I also saw the lightweight dark blue zip up hooded jacket that 'Paul' had been wearing during the murder scene.

"A few of these can be reused from one production to another," Ken said. "But they represent a certain investment. We do some trading too with other theater companies. You can see why. Occasionally we can find some helpful things at the Tuesday Market."

I saw an army uniform, one for a nurse, and several robes of indeterminate function. One of them was a black full-length cloak with a hood. It reminded me of the grim reaper, or something for one of the ghosts in *A Christmas Carol.* I focused more on the wigs spread across the top shelf on dummy head forms, but none of them was clown red. Hanging at the side wall of the cabinet was a sword in an elaborate scabbard. It had a long blade with a gradual curve. "Wouldn't this be considered a prop?" I said. "It looks lethal."

"Yes, and it is, by the way, but the prop cabinet is too short to accommodate it, so it has to stay here. Anyway, that's about all there is. It's not much to create new worlds out of, but somehow it still works most of the time. Fortunately, people are easily engaged if they allow themselves to be. They cooperate in their deception. The ones that don't never show up at the theater."

"What I see here is that the San Miguel Theater Company is an association of improvisers with a new reality, even though the book they work from is rigid. But that's only their starting point, so you can call them dream producers. They're storytellers before all else. Coming together this time they were acting out before the world a story called *Identity Crisis*."

"Exactly, first lived by you and your associates, but then raised by them to the level of art."

"It started as my story, yet I can also see a subtext in this production. Take any play: *Macbeth, Julius Caesar, Death of a Salesman*, or *After the Fall. Who's Afraid of Virginia Woolf?* They all have a subtext."

Ken looked at me doubtfully. "You're right about that, they often do, but I've been through this playbook backward and forward. It's mainly a mystery and a rather violent one, focused on an environmental disaster. It may be too real to have a subtext, since it was not based on art, only facts. Have I somehow missed something?

You're the investigator."

As a painter, I understood this. "I feel like I have too at this point. Talk to your playwright, Rodrigo Ferrer. Ask him what the play meant to him. You have more to lose here than I do, and since you've been working closely with him, he may talk more easily with you before he talks to me. Although, he will still have to talk to me to solve this."

As I walked back through the lobby out onto the clearer atmosphere of Avenida Independencia I paused under the overhang with the growing sense that I was missing something, not an unusual feeling so early in an investigation. It was natural that Rodrigo Ferrer would've made our own case report into theater art in his own way, according to his own vision. But I also knew one thing more—that the subtext Ken had missed must've been *revenge*, an element that had never entered into the real case we'd filed four years ago as *Identity Crisis*.

CHAPTER SIX

We allowed a full day to pass to give Simone Garfield a chance to settle down emotionally, surely not nearly enough, knowing she would still never fully recover. Unintentionally killing a fellow actor onstage would throw anyone into a spiral of turmoil and self-doubt. It was not at all like hitting a pedestrian that blindly ran out between parked cars into her path, since in this case there was no way to attach the slightest blame, like carelessness, to the victim. Rebecca had been neither careless nor naive. Certainly the first of Simone's days of recovery would've been partly occupied by Delgado's second round of questioning. We knew, at least, that he had found no reason to hold her overnight, but that could be reversed at any time as easily as changing his mind. We had seen that on other cases, and our need to sort this one out in real terms was growing by the hour.

Maya and I drove out to Simone's place in the La Lejona neighborhood on the southern edge of San

Miguel. It was in the area behind la Comer, the supermarket that used to be named Mega. What we were looking for was a sense of who the victim had been and what, if any, relationship she'd had with Simone. In the play they had discarded the name of Mercy Buchanan because that was the real name of the woman in our case, and we had made it a condition of Rodrigo Ferrer using our files that no real names would be used other than ours in the Agency and Diego Delgado's. As a prosecuting investigator Delgado was a public figure, and he had no immunity from publicity. He would've been the last one to try to claim it; I'd always thought he enjoyed his intermittent moments in the spotlight. In the real case, Maya had shot Mercy Buchanan dead when she reached for her gun as we walked into our bed and breakfast room in Guanajuato. When art imitates life, it can sometimes come uncomfortably close.

The young actress who had died playing her was really named Rebecca Carson. In the playbill they hadn't given the character a last name. This had all been the decision of the playwright, Rodrigo Ferrer, who had known her slightly, as I'd heard from someone secondhand, and he'd proposed her for the part. As the playwright, he owned some degree of control, including casting, and the rest had mostly rested in the hands of Ken Fairfax in his role as director, and in a larger sense, the owner of the theater company.

The building where Simone Garfield lived was a light green two-story structure at the intersection of Calles Obregón and Braganza. La Lejona is not a historic neighborhood in the way many others are here in San Miguel. It's not more than twenty-five or thirty years old, and most of the houses appeared to be on the rim of middle class and holding. Simone's was a well-kept rendition of the traditional style with an ample stone cornice at the roofline and tall windows framed in buff-colored limestone on both floors. The ones on the street level were barred with elegant ironwork. That was typical and I took it as a sign that the apartments within were well cared for.

As the actual shooter I was especially eager to speak with Simone Garfield. In other cases we never saw the shooter until the end, if at all. Maya and I stared at each other for a moment on the front step before I rang the upper of two bells. On a paper tab beneath the button, set high on the doorframe away from the reach of children, were the letters S. GARFIELD in blue ink, their edges now blurry from humid weather.

Maya must've been wondering what it was going to be like to meet the actor who played her onstage. Knowing this meeting was coming, she and I had never talked about what the actors who played us might really be like in their own skin. It was better to have no expectations on how someone else could reach into her psyche and come up with Maya, a woman she had never met. I had Lance Bitman ('Paul') on my schedule, but the meeting wouldn't happen until that afternoon, when, I hoped, we would be more prepared.

A silent pause followed. It was a bright morning at about eleven o'clock. I had made this appointment with Simone by email, and I had never spoken to her, even on the stage as I picked up the gun she'd dropped at her feet. At that moment, in the presence of the dead girl on the bed, a person she had just killed, Simone was beyond all reason, and there was hardly anything that could be said to her that she would've heard. I recall thinking I might have to break her fall if she fainted, that I needed to be ready to catch her by her armpits, but how would that go if she fell forward, away from me? Everything was moving too quickly even as it felt frozen in time. I didn't believe I could get in front of her soon enough to keep her face from hitting the stage. These are some of the silly things you recall about a horrifying moment of crisis like that.

A second later the interior bolt slid back with a clang and the door swung open.

The woman inside looked like she hadn't been able to decide who she was going to be that day. She wore a blue pullover sweater above a long, billowy white muslin skirt of several layers. Her nearly black, wavy hair was parted in the center and pulled forward over her shoulders. I recalled how it had been elaborately coiled at both sides onstage. If she was wearing any makeup it was too subtle to detect, although her eyes seemed slightly shadowed. Her wide, mobile mouth had a downward curl that did not look normal, but that was only a guess. Her jaw was firm and strongly defined. A pair of charming dimples was not enough to offset her stressed manner.

Allowing for that, I found her features appealing and bold enough to make a large variety of statements onstage, even at some distance from the audience. Maya had suggested from the playbill headshot photo that she was about thirty-five or six, but seeing her face to face it seemed she was more like thirty-one or two. She was about three inches taller than Maya, who is five-foot-six.

Naturally we had seen a great deal of Simone in the first half of the play. Maya had wanted her character to be played by a Mexican woman, but the audience was almost entirely expatriates. The choices were therefore limited, since the play was performed in English, which is common enough here among the local Mexicans as a second language, but rarely at a sufficient level to act in a play.

"Paul and Maya," she said, shaking her head with an ironic twist to her lips. "I know those names almost better than my own now. You've become real people to me, so I will continue to dream about you forever. Please come in." She stepped back and gestured to a flight of stairs to the right of another doorway inside. We started walking up behind her. "And please excuse the way everything looks this morning. I haven't been able to get my act together yet. I don't know whether to drink more wine or less. To tell you the truth, I don't even know what day it is now. I don't know half the things I thought I knew before this happened."

"I'm sure," Maya said, as we approached the landing at the top. "Do you have any family here that could help you get through this?"

"No, they're all back in Rhode Island, where things like this don't happen. I haven't even called them because I don't feel like I can tell them yet about Rebecca. They've always hated the idea of me living in México. This is just going to prove everything they want to believe about this place, everything they ever said to me when I saw them at holidays, everything they said when I originally left, only now they'll be surprised that I'm not the one who's lying there dead on a slab in the morgue. That's their constant fear. Next I'll be in jail. That will not surprise them either."

I wondered silently whether Rebecca's parents were thinking the same thing, or something close to it. We entered a large well-lit room where one of the two narrower walls was entirely faced with mirrors. The floors were polished hard maple, which you rarely see in México, the ceilings were tall at about five meters, and the long wall facing the courtyard was mostly filled with windows. It gave an optimistic mood to the scene.

"It's a dance studio!" Maya said in a charmed voice, which immediately dropped a tone or two. "But the ballet bar is gone."

"Yes it is, but I can still hear those girls dancing," Simone said, her fingers moving in fluttery patterns. "It's very subtle but it's all nevertheless happening here in this room. Even now. Even at this moment, with you here." She looked around, listening. "It's a subtle presence, you know? But very real, more than the rest of this."

I studied her posture as she spoke. This was not the first time reality had come up in this case. Simone's shoulders were curved slightly inward, and her hands tended to be protective of her breast when she wasn't gesturing. Thin curved lines bracketed both sides of her mouth like a pair of fine parentheses that gave her speech a tiny degree of emphasis. Maya and I sat down on one of two worn but clean sofas set at a right angle to each other. Across the room toward the street wall, two tables were piled with swatches and fabric remnants. A third held a sewing machine, and against the same wall stood a dressmaker's form. Simone Garfield must've made her own costumes for the stage. I tried to recall how she'd been dressed that night without much success.

"We won't take up a lot of your time today," said Maya, "and I know how difficult and unfair this has been for you." She paused for a moment, but Simone only nodded without more response. "I can also see that acting in a play with other people is like being part of a new family. You quickly form attachments and loyalties. You adopt the feelings and emotions of the part you're playing. You're connected in the relationships, like with 'Paul.' It's sounds funny to call him that after the way it ended. Now, without seeing that part onstage as it developed in your script, you've had a sudden loss."

Simone looked at her for a long moment. "So you've worked in theater before?"

Maya shook her head gently. "No, but every case we've taken has had a piece of theater in it. You can't escape it. People act out roles they've created to escape from the crimes they committed. If they survive, the victims invent roles of escape. Our role is always to be the hunters. The script is the same and we always play ourselves."

"I can see that. That makes it easier to improvise, then, doesn't it? Theater happens everywhere. You've heard the term street theater, but there is also home theater, corporate theater, and government theater. It goes on and on."

"All the world's a stage," I said with no irony, meaning to move on from Theater Theory 101. "I had hoped you could tell us something about Rebecca as a person, even if it's not the best time to be talking about her."

"Well, yes, Rebecca Carson." Simone's face took on a weary cast. "As much as I liked her in the way you'd want to encourage a young actor starting out, she was still a little green. That would be the same for anyone of her age and experience." Simone's lips grew tight as if she were struggling for control.

"We're a little green here too," said Maya, smiling softly, as if extending a hand, but she stopped short of that. "We've only had eighteen cases, so that's why we're so much in need of your help today. I hope you'll cut us the same degree of slack that you did with Rebecca."

I don't think Simone caught the unintended irony of this statement.

"Of course," she said. "As always."

"What was Rebecca's relationship with the other cast members?" I asked.

Simone sat nodding, with her hands locked together palm to palm between her knees in that ample skirt. "Naturally she was uncertain of her position with the rest of the more experienced people in the company. The theater crowd in this town is tightly knit without being entirely close. They can also be as cool to outsiders as they sometimes are to each other."

"Can you explain that a little more?" Maya said, nodding. To me, her smile was not quite credible.

"It's like you know everyone locally, except the

people who are occasionally brought in from New York or Los Angeles, but you're not always that eager to work with some of the other actors here. Maybe you've been cast with them before and it didn't work out that well. It happens, believe me."

"Does that come from a judgment about their level of skill?" I said, treating this as history more than supposition.

She nodded. "Skills, professionalism, and of course, ego is always part of it."

"Tell me more about ego. As a painter, I discovered long ago that ego has no part in that process, but maybe it's different in the theater."

She shook her head with a compressed look to her lips. "Anytime your ego enters before it's time to take your bow at the end, it's inappropriate. That's not just my view, other actors will tell you that too."

"Did Rebecca have a problem of that kind?" Maya said. "It seems like as the ingénue that could be a temptation. Wasn't she coming on to 'Paul' the whole time? In the story, I mean?"

That had been the situation in the real case, which had complicated the fact that Maya killed Mercy Buchanan. Maya's antennae were always finely tuned to vibrations of that kind.

It took Simone a moment to respond, and she started with a long sigh. "I think Rebecca was playing it the way she imagined she would play it in her own life. At that age she might've overplayed it, especially if 'Paul' was already attached to a woman a few years older than she was. Like me as 'Maya'." Simone paused and gazed off into the wall of mirrors. "But I'm only speculating, OK? You have to imagine that as I observed her in rehearsal I was more involved in creating my own 'Maya' role onstage."

Here she smiled weakly at Maya, who smiled back with no more definition.

"What's your range onstage?" I said, intentionally throwing out a curve ball question.

She gave me a frank look and took no time to think. "I can play anyone." I sensed that she had said this before during casting interviews.

"Even a man?"

"Yes, in a heartbeat, even a very strong man, or an elderly man, but maybe not an infant or an animal, or a bug."

"Good bug parts must be quite rare," I said, "and rightly so. You don't see much Kafka on stage these days. But how about a spirit? A benign sprite or a ghost, a sinister visitor?"

"Oh yes, no problem with any of those. I've seen *Poltergeist* five times."

"And how about a young Mexican woman detective?" said Maya, with no irony in her voice, but I knew she'd been waiting to ask this question.

Simone studied her for a moment, looking her in the eye. "As Rodrigo wrote that part, 'Maya' was not specifically Mexican, OK? But I was ready to play her that way. We chose not to."

"We?" I said.

With a small shrug Simone looked off through the windows. "Ken and I discussed it in some detail before we went to rehearsal. The name itself could've been American too, or several other things. He felt that making the character Mexican might make the part a bit unnatural and distract from other aspects of the 'Maya' character that he wanted to emphasize. Almost in the way that using a heavy dialect distracts from the action if you're not very careful. It's always better to just hint at dialect or accents."

Maya said nothing to this. She believed her English was as good as anyone's in the room, and she had no investment in the way people in a play might represent her way of speaking.

After a moment of silence, Simone added, "I mean, it's all just theater. At the beginning you only have a few lines to sketch things in, sometimes just one or two, and you can't make it too complicated."

"Who was Rebecca as an actor, really?" I said, thinking how complicated it had become.

Simone produced an apologetic smile. "I

recognized her accent right away. I mean, we were both from the same part of New England. I could understand how she'd been raised, what her values were, where she'd gone to school, and even more I could appreciate how she was trying to establish herself in the theater community here, by inching up to the men who ran it."

"Did you resent that?" Maya said, harmlessly.

"Not at all, not at all. In San Miguel we're always struggling to find young women who can fill the ingénue roles. Some are like her and some are not, but the range of choices is never wide. So if you come down here at that age and you don't have your own money, then you have to find some work, and being an actor usually pays only slightly better than being a poet. Not always, of course. A few of us here do fairly well."

Nodding slowly, I could see that. Most painters find themselves only a notch or two higher on that pay scale. At least as a poet you'd be self-employed, always a plus for me too, since I'd never been able to take orders. "How well did the other people in this theater company accept her?"

Simone thought for a moment as if trying to phrase her answer to create the right impression. For an instant I saw her as being a bit too careful, but we'd seen that before in a myriad of interviews like this one. It could easily be an instinctive response, and she was already in a very difficult position.

"Ken has already told you about that, I'm sure."

"Yes, but we don't like to only talk to one person in cases like this."

"OK, that gets into some local politics. I want to say that not everyone in this town lets you in the door right away on the day you show up, you know? Most of us who've found our place here struggled to locate an entry point in this business, since you have to prove yourself as part of the admission process. Being young and cute isn't enough, especially when many of your judges are middle aged or older women who've lost the charm of their youthful good looks. They're struggling to find other roles when they want to stay involved in theater, and many of them do. That's not fair to either group, but it's real. You'll find a number of successful women directors and producers now, but no one gets a free pass, here or anywhere, on either end of the process. As an artist yourself, Paul, you must already know this."

"Where are you in that process?" said Maya, with no guile. The back and forth motion of her extended index finger appeared to draw a line in the sand, or at least on the hardwood floor. While Cody was our chief investigator, I thought Maya had been especially astute in this conversation.

"Without being an ingénue I am still young and cute, OK? That's why I was cast as 'Maya.'" Of course Simone knew she was not going to get any disagreement with this.

"Is the casting couch ever a part of that?" I said, still thinking of stage politics.

Simone shook her head firmly. "This is not at all like Hollywood. Maybe that happens on Broadway, but I've never gotten close to Broadway, or even off-Broadway, so I don't think so. It's more like that old saw, payin' your dues. In the music business it's called scuffling."

"How did Rebecca pay her dues?" said Maya, quick to seize on this idea. "It sounds like she found herself between the sword and the wall."

"You're right. For every newcomer it starts with not getting much respect. You're the last to do your makeup, even if you're onstage in the opening scene. There are only two tables with mirrors in the dressing room. Your costume is fitted last. You may be cast first just because ingénues are hard to find, but in the playbill credits your name and photo are at the bottom of the page."

"And Rebecca's costume in act three was a bed sheet," I said.

Simone gave me a long look. "Yes, well, and a used one. The wardrobe budget is often tight, especially in a three-day production like this. There was some double stick tape for her in there somewhere, but it must have come loose in the end. I feel terrible for Rebecca, and even for myself, but after I stood there onstage and screamed, I also suddenly felt that this had been a long time in coming."

"That's an interesting statement. Did she deserve it in some way?" Maya said.

"Never! That's not what I meant." This was like a small eruption followed by a moment of awkward silence.

"Then what did that mean?" I said.

"It's mainly the irony of it, I suppose. She hired on for the ingénue victim role and became the ingénue victim in real life."

I could see from the look on Maya's face that she regarded this idea as being too much like fate, a popular concept in México and one she despised.

"Can we go over the journey of the gun that killed her?" I said. "I know you must've gone back and forth on this point with the police."

Simone nodded firmly as if she knew we'd also be going over this part of the story again. "The first I saw of it was during the intermission. At that point the purse was on the prop table at backstage center along with some other things, I don't recall what now. I had already changed and come out of the dressing room."

"Do you recall who else was in the area?" said Maya.

"The stage manager, of course, his first name is Alfonso and now I can't recall his last name. He's an instructor of Rodrigo's at the university. Lance was there as 'Paul', still changing in the dressing room. Rebecca was standing behind him wrapped up in her sheet. 'Delgado' was also there waiting for a later cue, and a couple of others. I can't think who else now. A minute before the confusion started I saw Ken backstage on the other side, down where the prop cabinet and the supplies and tools are. They call it the dungeon."

"The *confusion* started?" I said, more coolly than I felt. "What was that about? Isn't that the last thing you want during a performance?"

"Well yes, and it was only three or four minutes before Lance and I were supposed to go out to the lobby to make our entrance down the left aisle from there, and suddenly the zipper on Lance's hooded jacket got jammed in the dressing room. I don't know if it was already jammed when he took it out of the wardrobe closet, but he didn't have it on yet, and he couldn't get it on. Usually if you could get it off all right it wouldn't have been jammed, and you wouldn't jam it just by hanging it up, either. It wasn't right, you know?"

"What happened then?" I was going to ask if the jacket was really an essential part of playing that scene, but Lance and Ken having thought so was enough.

"Everybody rushed in and gathered around the jacket trying to help. We all felt under the gun. Rebecca wasn't doing much because she was kind of precariously dressed, but the others were hovering over it. Lance had it in his hands, and Nicole Landfair, the prop mistress, was pulling on it too. Alfonso, the stage manager, was there bent over it. I was behind them and up the steps so I couldn't see very well what was happening."

"But they did get it cleared?" said Maya.

"Yes, but only after a couple minutes of tension. Then Lance finally pulled it on and we went back to the prop table. Rebecca went up to assume her place onstage. Nicole Landfair showed me the gun inside the purse before I picked it up, and Lance and I walked down the covered side aisle to the lobby. By that time the audience was all seated again and we'd only lost a couple of minutes, maybe three or four."

Maya and I looked at each other. "Could the live bullet have been added to the gun during that time of confusion?"

"It was a panicky moment, of course, but at least it wasn't in the middle of a scene, when someone had to make an entrance at a precise moment, on cue. The audience would never have noticed the time we lost. Sometimes it can be hard to get them reseated anyway. But I suppose the gun could've been tampered with when people were crowded into the dressing room." She put her right hand over her mouth for a moment and looked at the floor as if seeing all this again.

"But you didn't notice anyone at the prop table?"

"Well, no one but the prop mistress, but like everyone, I was paying attention to the zipper crisis. No one was looking back toward the prop table. And remember, the dressing room is about five steps down from the backstage level, and Lance was standing close to the wardrobe doors, so not everyone around him could've seen the prop table even if they'd looked back up in that direction. From what I recall, no one did. Why would they?"

We paused for a while. Simone raised her eyebrows as if she was glad to have gotten through an unavoidable part of the conversation, one she'd been dreading.

I leaned forward from my place on the sofa. "So who would've wanted to kill Rebecca enough to set this up? Because it doesn't sound to me that the jammed zipper could've been an accident. We've all had jammed zippers, and that one seems frivolous, like it had no cause except to provide an opportunity for an unnoticed person to tamper with the gun."

Simone Garfield leaned forward as well, shaking her head. "As it happened, if those two things are really connected. I don't envy either of you your task in this. The theater is a framework for illusion. If it's repertory, then I am this character tonight and I am that one tomorrow. Perhaps I am really neither, or both. It's always about multiple identities, which implies multiple truths."

Maya was not put off by this as much as I was, although I understood it. "I think we're used to that by now. Then who was Rebecca?" she said.

Simone leaned back in her chair. "By the night of the opening she was playing herself more than any of the rest of us were. That's all I know. That's all I ever knew. Remember, since you saw all her lines in the play, Rebecca was never at the center of the action. She was more like a sideshow; an ongoing tease to distract 'Paul,' and the story was much more about the two of you. The truth of this murder may lie within yourselves, and Rodrigo Ferrer might never have gotten at it. Did he ever talk to you about the case in detail? About what it all really meant to him? Or did he only use the facts as he found them in the case record?"

"He never did confer with us," I said. "I always felt that he wanted to develop the motivations and characters without our input, although he did record our voices several times to get the tone and style of our delivery right."

"I really do wish I had more to give you," Simone said, leaning back in her chair gripping both her shoulders. "To be utterly honest, I also wish I could find something in this disaster for myself, something to learn from a terrible mistake that I didn't plan on making or foresee in any way."

A few minutes later Maya and I left with the

thought that there had been a second play being performed that night, and not all the actors had been working from the same script.

CHAPTER SEVEN

Lance Bitman, the actor who had played 'Paul Zacher,' readily agreed to meet with me, but he wanted to see my studio in our house on Quebrada, so I agreed to do the conversation there. He arrived about four in the afternoon of the same day we'd talked with Simone Garfield, and Maya led him upstairs. She thought it better if she left the conversation to us. It would be Paul versus 'Paul,' she'd said before he arrived, but I knew she was still ruminating about Simone. I was too.

"Lance," I said, standing up with my hand outstretched as he came in. My tone was that of old college buddies, meeting again after eighteen years. I'd been painting earlier between interviews, after our conversation with Simone, but I'd cleaned up around three-thirty. I was still sitting at the easel, examining my progress, when he came in. "Thanks for coming today." His grip was loose and approximate, his movements elastic. I was relieved that it didn't at all feel like I was shaking hands with myself. My own grip was firmer and more direct. I was suddenly glad he didn't know that much of the detail of being Paul Zacher.

Facing him now in my studio I realized he was no more than five-foot-eight in height, and lightly framed. This made him nearly five inches shorter than I was. Still, I had to give him credit for the fact that I hadn't noticed it onstage. His face was not remarkable, not in any way a standout, but with the right makeup and lighting he could've portrayed a lot of different types of men. He looked like he was in his late thirties.

For a moment his eyes traveled over the painting I'd been working on. It was a sister portrait of two women born in San Miguel to expat parents. They were both now in their forties and had grown up here and married Mexican men. In the pose they were facing each other in profile. The negative space between their faces was a perfect study in form.

"That's wonderful," he said. "They're so alike, yet very different."

"That's what interested me about them. It's nearly finished now, I'm only touching up the background and some other details, and tweaking a few highlights. They each plan to have it hanging over their mantel six months of the year."

"I wish I had seen this before we started rehearsing. It would've given me some valuable insights into how you work."

"Well, Lance, we just didn't have a chance to do that. I was busy, and to tell you the truth, we didn't think to offer that to the actors. Neither Maya nor I had any concept of how the players would prepare for a role, and we were trying to be accepting of whatever Rodrigo Ferrer came up with. He never showed us the script when it was finished, and we hadn't asked to see it."

He nodded solemnly. "Paul, please call me Paul," he said.

"...OK, but that's not your name, is it? I'm Paul Zacher."

He shrugged as if this didn't matter. "Neither is Lance my real name. It's Lawrence, but I like to lose myself in the character I'm playing at the moment, you know? Live the role. Get into the character's shoes and walk down the street as that person, elbowing some people out of the way and shaking hands with others. Make them remember you."

He waited for me to respond, but I didn't.

"I also wish I could've sat down then in this chair in front of your easel for a while. It's my own style of method acting, OK? All these smudges of paint tell me something. You can pull any hat off the rack, put it on, and that's your takeoff point. It's the same as walking through a door. As I can see now, your particular hat has a lot of detail on it."

"Thank you." Was that a compliment? I did have a collection of hats but I didn't think any of them said the same thing about me. They were more about different moods than multiple personalities. I looked at Lance for a moment, but found no way to get into his train of thought. He was surveying the contents of the studio, the other furniture, and the three recent paintings leaning against the cabinet wall to dry.

"Lance Bitman is a career role," he continued, "a lifestyle, a profession, a leading part. But like everyone else the audience sees onstage, Lance Bitman is not a real person." He said this with a tilt to his head that I read as self-indulgent.

"Sure, but that particular play is over now, Lance. The run has been cancelled early because of that young woman's death."

"You mean Rebecca."

"Yes, *Lance*."

"*Paul*."

Now I was starting to feel I had made a mistake by letting him come to my studio. It's a private place where I do my most important work. Even if he could mimic me sitting there, it didn't mean he understood what I did when I painted. I didn't always understand it myself. It wasn't something that needed to be understood in order to function; it often ran beneath the surface of consciousness, in whatever you wish to call that space.

"Look, Lance, or whoever you are today. I thought you did a good job as Paul Zacher, as me, but now all that's over, OK? We're not speaking our lines here anymore. This is my studio, so we're telling the facts as we saw them. When I pick up a brush and apply paint to the canvas, there's nothing equivocal about that, OK? It's a commitment."

"I can see that."

"The 'Paul' of the play was a detective. There is not one painting scene in Identity Crisis. I've gone back to being the only Paul Zacher in this town now, and I'd like to keep it that way. We won't be giving Rodrigo Ferrer access to our files again. There's been no discussion of a sequel, and there won't be. Now let's talk about how you assembled your idea of me."

Early on when we were working with Rodrigo, I had guessed that it might be difficult to see someone play me onstage, but this was worse than I thought, since he was now trying to play me offstage as well. I had never anticipated that a character would seep under the theater doors and spread into the real world like a genetically altered virus.

"OK, I got it now, I got it. You're going to be the director! Only I wish I had seen your studio before. Think of all the marvelous props! The paint-spattered easel, those rolls of fresh canvas still smelling of primer, that rack of stretchers over there in the corner. The two vases full of brushes, upright on their handle ends. It's all real, you know, all of it right down to your shoes."

Involuntarily I looked down at them. They were my most comfortable painting shoes, with an almost iconic presence. In the theater they would've been the perfect props. They were old leather high-tops to keep the paint off my socks, and on their spattered surface I could still pick out elements of specific paintings. They were part of my history, even of my artistic development, and they were at least ten years old. Maya hated them. When I glanced in turn at his feet Lance saw my look. He was wearing a pair of tired loafers artificially flecked with drops of house paint. They reminded me of a cheap mobile Jackson Pollock copy.

"I suppose you wore those onstage." It had never occurred to me to look at his feet.

"Of course. They were fundamental to my performance, almost the foundation of it. I talked before about getting into your shoes."

I didn't want to mention my own cabinet full of painting props; interesting items for still lifes, and outfits for models. "Call me Paul," I said firmly. "It's time to hang up our costumes."

Lance frowned as if that was going too far. "I don't think I can. You're not that real to me as Paul. You didn't prove it before when we started rehearsal. You could've given me some bit of business that brought you alive as

Paul Zacher the sleuth. A tiny notebook, for example, or a battered trench coat. You could've been chewing on a cigar stub that you never lit. Or you could've been blind in one eye, but still seeing a crime scene better than anyone else, you know? You can't imagine how hard I worked just to bring you alive at all. As a character, you're not that easy. I wanted to be gesturing with a paintbrush in the first half, but the director couldn't figure out where to put an easel onstage. All the props were too sketchy, he said. No pun intended."

"I'm sure." I leaned back in my chair and for a long moment searched for a reason to continue with this charade. I felt like I was now in a play myself, that this meeting had somehow been scripted on his side, but I was still improvising a role I didn't understand as well as I thought, even though I'd been playing a painter for twenty-five years. I decided to struggle on.

"Now I'm trying to see how you could become a painter onstage. Maybe it doesn't lie in some gesture you picked up from me; you might have to find the elements of it within yourself. Aren't you, *Lance*, to some degree, every character you play?"

"Good job! Now we're making some progress here."

"Right. Demonstrating all this artsy stuff is new to me. Normally I just go home and paint after cases like this, sitting in this chair, but without having to think about what I'm doing. It just comes to me."

As Lance looked at me more seriously, lines creased his forehead. "You're saying it's more private, kind of an inward thing." A shaky gesture of his right hand suggested how vague this sounded to him.

I nodded. "That's where I find it. But because it comes more from the right brain, and therefore the less verbal side, I've never theorized much about it, so it's hard to discuss it now. But tell me more about Rebecca. What was your reaction when you saw she'd really been shot?"

He shook his head. "It took me a moment. There was a tiny lag before I realized it was real. It got me almost searching for a line I didn't have. You don't expect to find anything *real* onstage, you know? That's why we're not having this conversation there. I had seen Rebecca seeming to get shot a number of times before in rehearsals. It was only at the end that we used real blanks in the dress rehearsal, but this was suddenly very different."

"Until then you were intentionally deceiving the audience."

"No!" He took a quick step back from me. "We were helping them to create a new reality in their minds. But when Rebecca was thrown back onto the pillows like that, it was like being in rehearsal again and she had made the wrong move, because it wasn't what 'Maya' and I thought she was going to do. Reality rushed in, like if the director had walked onstage and said, 'That doesn't work for me, Lance. Do it like this next time.'"

"The illusion was shattered."

"Right. It fell to the stage like broken glass."

Those words had a familiar ring. "Even for you" I said, "because at that moment, the real Paul Zacher acting as himself in a drama based on his own case would've jumped into his investigation mode. Trust me on this."

"Crossover points," Lance said after a moment of thought. He nodded with a weary look as if this was old news. "We don't have those crossover points onstage. You're either working from the book or you're not. There can't be two simultaneous illusions, so you never go back and forth, unless it's a French drama and something very avant-garde. You'd never see that in this town, of course. In New York they can do anything, but here people want to understand what they're looking at. That's their weakness."

"The book is the script."

"Yes, invariably. The book always rules."

"Did you see at that instant, or just before that second shot that killed Rebecca, any other action onstage or backstage that didn't quite fit the play, the book as you call it?"

"As I *knew* it, top to bottom. But no, I didn't. I liked her, Rebecca, I really did. I knew she was green and her only experience had been some summer stock in Connecticut, maybe two productions, but I wanted her to do well in this scene. It was both the climax and the end of her part. What followed was all about the consequences of her death. The scenes that came next between 'Paul' and 'Maya' were the most substantial part of the play, because 'Maya' blamed 'Paul' for being forced to kill Rebecca, and she hated doing that more than anything."

I paused for a moment. That did reflect a painful reality for the Zacher Agency in the original case. "Rodrigo got that part absolutely right. How much did you like her personally, Rebecca, I mean offstage?"

He visibly edged several degrees back into his Paul Zacher role. Had the set of his chin changed? It did not appear to be drawn from the *Identity Crisis* script this time, but from another book, a subtler one, perhaps one in his head that had been launched backstage as a subtext. I made a note to talk again with Ken Fairfax about the relationship among the players. Overlaying this conversation upon the one with Simone earlier that day, I wondered how many plays were being performed simultaneously that night.

"I really just wanted Rebecca to do well, nothing more. She was a great kid and we artists all have to support each other, right?"

I've heard that before and I wished it was true, but I had rarely experienced it. Painters never cooperate with each other. Besides, *a great kid* seemed like a demeaning term to use for a young woman who had just been murdered. "And was she doing well?"

Lance shrugged as his glance wandered away. "She had the look of her character and the choreography of the scenes down. That's important, because Ken hates unscripted movement onstage. He's one of those theater guys who believes everything has to mean something, or it's wasted. His approach is that he has an economical frame of mind—if an action or a line doesn't contribute something to advance the action, it doesn't belong there."

"So she was doing well?" I repeated.

"Yes, generally, but I thought she was delivering her lines a bit too fast and not projecting enough. To me, it felt like she wanted to quickly get out of the spotlight, almost to catch her breath. These are things you learn with experience; calmness and pace."

"How would you have helped her if you'd been directing?"

"I would've put her in the back row during some part of the rehearsal when she wasn't onstage and had her listen to the other players with a script in her lap, paying special attention to their timing and the way they projected their lines. She knew enough by that point to observe how they were doing it."

"Did Ken Fairfax do that?"

"No, but even late in rehearsals he took her aside

several times, out of earshot of the rest of us. From her look when she came back on, she may have felt singled out."

"How did Rebecca react to that?"

"Twice I saw her come back a little huffy, as if what Ken had told her didn't help her get into the role. My observation was that it made her feel more that it was about her personally, not her stage character. But it may have been more about her reaction than his comments. Ken has a ton of experience with actors, and he's a great one himself."

"And that must include managing wannabe actors," I said, "since this town is full of them. Directing has also been a big part of his career."

"Absolutely. I can't explain that tension any further. Maybe he's used to working with more experienced people. As you can imagine, there's a shortage of young English speaking actors in this community. So much of the expat population here is of retirement age. You don't want to be casting sixty-year-old women as ingénues. It makes everything a comedy."

"How well was 'Maya' doing during this performance, that is, before she fired the fatal bullet?"

He looked at me as if I should've known this, seated as I was in the front row. "As 'Maya' or any other character, Simone is always a pro. 'Maya' was not a tough role for her. Ice wouldn't melt in her mouth, even if she was wailing in a Greek tragedy. There is no actor in this town that I would rather work with. She's always there; she's always on point. Twice I've missed a cue with her and she's given my line to me under her breath without missing a beat."

"Was it in character for her to scream like that after the gun went off with a real round in the cylinder?"

Lance slowly exhaled with a grim smile, and started to rub his face with both hands. "Yes and no. I mean it did fit the action as we saw it, and as you saw in the audience, but it wasn't in the book. I had the sense later that she felt it was what the real Maya Sanchez would've done. That's the level of insight that she has."

I didn't respond directly to this because it wasn't true. "How about the crew and the rest of the cast? Does anyone look iffy to you?"

"Well, who can say? This was a hybrid production with people from that college in Guanajuato and some of the usual local talent. *Identity Crisis* was only going to run for three nights, so it was not the biggest deal in the world. If you ask me, I thought Ken was paying off an old favor to someone in the Guanajuato theater community by doing this play at all, since that short a run was never going to earn back its costs."

"Even less now."

Lance regarded me solemnly. "Yes, even less now."

"Tell me about the stuck zipper. Does this case turn on that moment?"

Both his hands went up in frustration, as his delivery grew more forceful. "That was one of those situations you absolutely cannot see coming. I was there in the dressing room, and we were on time and ready. The break was coming to an end, and Alfonso was five steps up glancing at his watch every ten seconds, checking on where everyone was."

"From where you were could you see him there?"

"I could mainly see his back."

"And you were certain it was him?"

"Absolutely. When he's nervous he has a funny stance with more weight on one foot than the other. Rebecca was arranging the double stick tape that held the sheet around the upper part of her body, because that was all she had, so my back was turned to her. All I needed for that scene was 'Paul's' zip up jacket with a hood. I pulled it out of the wardrobe cabinet and discovered the zipper was jammed."

"What did that tell you?"

As if looking back on that moment, Lance's face took on a shadowy reddish cast. "It said that someone was fucking with me during a performance! Can you imagine that? Nobody hates me that much! There was no way in hell that zipper could've been jammed. I mean, the last person couldn't have gotten it off if it had been jammed closed like that, right? So somebody had set me up. That's all I could figure."

"You'd worn it before?"

"Yes! I wore it the day before, at the dress rehearsal. I would've been the last one to wear it, so tell me how I managed to pull it off with a jammed zipper, and then left it that way in the wardrobe to screw myself up during opening night." Reading his face I could see nothing but genuine indignation.

"I do see your point, but who would be trying to trip you up? Was it someone in the cast? The crew? Someone who hates you?" I couldn't resist repeating that last possibility.

Uncharacteristically, Lance shrugged at this question and added nothing else, peering forward as if discovering an unnoticed element in the sinister group portrait of that moment, one he'd missed before.

"Lance, don't stop here. Think of yourself again as 'Paul Zacher' in the play, and now you're onto something important in this case. Who would wish you harm? Have you made any enemies during this production?"

He waved this idea off with a chuckle. "Surely not anyone in *Identity Crisis*."

I tried not to laugh myself. That case was the closest we had ever come to all of us in the Agency being murdered. But we were talking about two different things.

"But wouldn't such a person need to know the procedures backstage to set that up?"

"Yes, but what if it's something small that I did to alienate someone?" he said.

"What looks small to you might be big to someone else." I began to guess. "How about Rodrigo Ferrer? Did you offend him? I'm thinking that any actor might have."

"No, not in a heartbeat. That kid and I got on with each other big time."

"How about the one who played 'Delgado'?" I couldn't think of his name. Was it Ruben something?

"No, we clicked too."

"Alfonso, the stage manager?"

Lance was silent for a long moment. "No, his job and his reputation were both at stake. He came on like a professional. I just can't come up with anyone else in the cast, OK? Next I think you should have a conversation with Nicole Landfair, the prop mistress. She had control of that gun until she handed it off as it went into the purse 'Maya' used."

"So when did the real bullet that killed Rebecca go into the cylinder?"

"Again, she could tell you that better than I could, if at all. I have no idea."

"Nicole is not a student locally?" I hadn't seen her the night of the murder, and no one like her had come onstage when the action stopped. Suddenly this struck me as odd.

"No, she's an American, but she grew up in México, maybe from high school on. I think her father worked at the U.S. Embassy in the capital and her family is now here."

"How old is she?"

"Mid twenties, twenty-six maybe."

"Can you elaborate on her customary role?"

"Not with many specifics. She's usually there next to a table in the center backstage, but when I see her I'm always about to go on or just coming off and I have my own issues to deal with. Like my costume or makeup, or what is my next cue coming on or going off. If there's a prop for me going on, she has it ready as I pass. Then I hand it back to her coming off. That's all I know. Of course, most of us have worked with her before."

"How is her Spanish?"

"As far as I can tell it's perfect, she grew up bilingual."

"Did you have any props in this play?"

"Well, 'Paul' always has his own gun, of course. It was mainly there to be a visible threat as I was wearing it, until 'Paul' is forced to hand it over in the last act, which has its main symbolic value—he was defeated. He never draws it and points it at anyone."

I remembered this from the original case with

chagrin. Rodrigo had not spared us, and there was no reason he should. The case had been a lesson in risk mismanagement. "And if he had drawn it? Did you ever break it open to inspect the cylinder?"

"No, but the person it's pointed at gets to inspect it before it goes onstage. There was no need for that with mine this time. It never left my holster."

That statement made me think for a moment, since I had already heard in detail about that safety regulation from Ken. "So even though no one inspected the one you were carrying, Rebecca would've inspected 'Maya's' gun. Did you observe her doing that?"

His head shook with impatience. "No, but that's bedrock procedure and it's always enforced quite rigidly in this theater, and in fact, in every theater I've ever worked in."

"Are all those guns at the Play House different?"

Lance shook his head. "No, it's the exact opposite. Every single one is a .38 police special, rather old hardware that can be bought cheaply in retirement. I was told the theater has four of them. By having them all be the same make and model, there's no problem for the prop mistress to remember which kind of ammunition goes with which gun. You can see how you'd want to simplify things backstage as much as you can to avoid tragic mistakes."

I had already observed this in the prop cabinet,

but how had Lance noticed that?

"And of course, all the rounds are blanks," he finished.

"Sure, there would never be any need to have real rounds in the theater, would there?" I said.

"Right. None at all. That would be far too dangerous."

After I showed Lance out the door and pointed him in the direction of the Quebrada overpass to find a taxi on Canal at the steps below, I called Delgado and let it ring for a while. I hadn't seen him since the murder two days earlier and we'd had no opportunity then for a conversation. You'd think a crowd that size would provide a lot of witnesses for a police investigation, but it mostly only muddies the ground with a lot of random and over-stimulated footprints. Worse, everybody is comparing notes before they talk to the police, so all the first impressions get merged and blurred. Defense attorneys know this well and they love it. Prosecutors hate it.

Although parking was still sparse, the traffic was nonexistent on Quebrada as I paused and leaned against my doorframe after Lance disappeared down the street. The bright and benevolent afternoon showed how fine October can be, but I could imagine a subtle cloud was still hanging over the theater on Independencia. Ken was a guy for whom control mattered, and Rebecca's murder must've been making him crazy every time he thought about it.

When Delgado picked up he went through his usual litany of opening gambits. Maya and her horse were both doing well, I responded as part of this ritual. "So I am guessing you have found yourself on this case now?" he said, finally. A note of resignation was audible in his voice.

"Yes. The theater company feels betrayed and blindsided, and there are some insurance issues as well."

"That I can understand. I have not said to them that it was such a carelessness to let this live bullet into their process, but that is what I have felt in my heart since I saw the victim. So young for the Señorita Rebecca Carson to die in that way. In any case, we shall leave the blame making to the court. And by the way, thank you for preserving that gun for us in its condition as a virgin to the crime."

"As always, that was my first goal." But what did that mean? "Did you get any good prints other than those of Simone Garfield?"

"We are still working through that, but we have hers, certainly. I will tell you more as it develops."

"Do you have a good suspect?"

"No. In our belief here in the Judicial Police, there are no good suspects."

I nodded patiently. "That is to say, do you have suspects you think might be guilty?"

"Not at this time."

"Not even Simone Garfield? I saw her pull the trigger. Everyone did."

"That is the problem, so no again. She is like a too obvious trick to be played upon us, and we are so much smarter than that, as you well know from the many cases we have shared. It is insulting to me to think that I might be expected to arrest her. Someone was seeking revenge on this woman, who is perhaps not the brightest we have ever encountered. In her past we may yet find an answer of who could hate her so much. For example, has she humiliated anyone at some other time?"

From the descriptions of theater politics we'd collected, that was more than possible.

"Did she admit that to you?"

"No, she said that if she had, she was not aware of it, because we have asked that to her more than once."

I wasn't ready to tell him we had already talked to her. "That may be. We are still in the early phases of this, and I'm anxious to talk with the students and faculty from Guanajuato before they go back home." That city, the capital of our state of the same name, was a little more than an hour's drive away. Like San Miguel, it was another colonial gem.

"There will be no problem for you with that," Delgado said. "I have since yesterday ordered them all to remain here in San Miguel, or I will come after them and arrest them as witnesses to be held in the *carcel* until the trial. Some have said I was making an ocean from a glass of water, but I have my job to do, as you know so well, and more than most, even."

"All right. Can I trouble you for the local address of the prop mistress, Nicole Landfair?"

"No problem again. But do you see for the others, it is now the same address for them all? The people of Guanajuato are staying at a bed and breakfast on Cuesta del Sol. The owner gave them a bargain rate since we are between the tourist seasons. He is also my cousin, Jorge Delgado Ruiz." As he gave me the address I could hear the smile in his voice.

"OK, but while Nicole Landfair is young, she is not from the university."

This must've raised Delgado's eyebrows. He rarely slipped up on detail. I heard pages shuffling. "Wait, here she is." He gave me an address in the gated Aldea community, just off the Ancha de San Antonio, and a phone number. I signed off with thanks.

A voice message had come in from Ken Fairfax while I was talking to Delgado. He had given Rebecca's parents, Drew and Diana Carson, my cell phone number. They had just arrived in town in a state of considerable distress. While that was totally understandable, he still hoped we wouldn't mind meeting with them. I could feel free to put it on his tab.

Or half tab, I thought, sharing the same ground as the insurance company, if for different reasons. I would be running interference. I phoned him back and said we'd be happy to take their call when it came in.

CHAPTER EIGHT

For a while after Delgado's call I stood thinking about Lance. His visit had not told me much about actors in general, but a great deal about his specific insecurities. I found it hard to believe that Ken Fairfax thought he was a good fit for me. Was it only the narrow range of choices he had available? Maybe like Maya's concern with Simone's portrayal of her, I ought to just let it go.

Half an hour later Cody came over for a briefing. Maya hadn't heard any of my conversation with the actor who'd played me, so we adjourned to the loggia behind the house at the edge of the garden.

I didn't say much about Lance's attitude, only that he'd struggled without much success to find a way into my thought process and character. He also felt he'd lacked the proper props and he'd discovered no information about my physical mannerisms in the case file. We went on to talk about the stuck zipper, which from its appearance in both the Simone and Lance interviews, was taking on increasing importance in the case.

"This opens out the field," Maya said. "Who was present for the zipper and who was not will give us the group of suspects."

Cody nodded. "Absolutely. I think the key is going to be who was absent from the dressing room during the attempt to free the jammed zipper. As we have more conversations let's try to place everyone during that time."

"But there's also the unlocked door at the side entrance to that small patio," I said, "which was always kept open during a performance to meet fire exit regulations, even if the sidewalk gate was locked. It was a way to at least get outside in an emergency."

"So if everyone backstage ran to the dressing room, some other unconnected party could still enter from the patio at that moment and add a live bullet to the gun," Maya said.

"Right," I said, "although if someone were coming in like that it would raise an alarm instantly if spotted, while anyone in the cast or crew hanging back might not, or wouldn't be noticed as anything out of the ordinary if he was. Then you have to ask, who was able to notice a stranger at that moment?"

"And," Cody said, "one other problem with that is how an outsider would know that was the precise time to enter. Theater is all about cues and timing, and he would have to know the exact moment when Lance tried to pull on the hooded jacket, without being able to coordinate it with him. I have to discount that idea based on the timing. It would have to be just too precise in order to work. Anyway, he could not see into the dressing room from out in the patio, even if the door were fully open. I checked out the sight lines there myself."

"And with that precise timing," I added, "how could the intruder have known to come over the wall at that moment? Because he wasn't coming in through the gate at the sidewalk."

"So then we're back now to those who were inside the backstage area." Maya had brought out a notepad and started a list of everyone who was backstage during the break. Out among the bromeliads lining the garden paths I glimpsed a subtle flutter, a flash of shiny black in the dim ground lights. They were there to provide ambiance more than guidance. This would be Orlando, our resident garden grackle. A longtime tenant, he had attended many of our conferences in the past, more as observer than contributor, and more in search of dropped snack items than for wine or information.

"Lance Bitman and Simone Garfield are there, of course, posing as us." Maya said, reading. "Ken Fairfax, the director."

"But I saw him outside, too," I said. "He was working the crowd during the break, just before we went in, even if that was only for a moment or two. I can't say how long he was out there."

"Was 'Cody' in the dressing room?" said Cody.

"We didn't hear that he was," I said, "and his cue for that opening scene in the second half came later, after Rebecca was killed."

Del Rupert, a Canadian whose father had been in the RCMP, had appeared as 'Cody.' With his blunt good humor he'd been able to get the manner right, although he lacked the proper height and mass.

Maya went back to her list. "We know from Simone that Alfonso, the stage manager was there, just up the steps."

"And Lance verified that when I talked to him."

"And we'll talk to him directly to verify that again. But how about Rodrigo Ferrer, the playwright?" I said. "When we talked to her, Simone didn't mention him as being present and neither did Lance when I talked to him."

"I didn't see him in the audience," Cody said, "although you'd think he'd sure as hell be there for his first opening night. Let's look into that further."

"Then there's the prop mistress, Nicole Landfair, a key figure in this," I said. "She's the gatekeeper, if she was doing her job."

"Then I think she's next on our list," Maya said.

"Damn!" yelled Cody, leaping up and raising his

left knee. We both looked at him in alarm. Was it some kind of cardiac event? Had he come to a breakthrough point in his mind? "That little fart under the table just pecked my ankle with that nasty beak of his. I think he made a hole in my sock." He leaned over and pulled up his pants cuff. Orlando had bolted back into the ground cover with a muted squawk.

"We've been ignoring that little guy, *qué lástima.* What a shame!" Maya went inside to collect some of the unsalted *pepitos*, the pumpkin seeds we saved for his visits. He hopped out into her path when she returned. Over the years in our garden, he'd not only owned the bug collection franchise, which was lushly rewarding, but the food scraps as well. With a burnished quality to his feathers, he looked well fed and prosperous, and in the way he cocked his head, quite intelligent. I saw him as an Orson Welles type among the local birds. *Shrewd* was the term often I thought of looking at him, even more so than many of our suspects, where *desperate* was more usually the term that came to mind.

"Ruben Gonzalez," Cody said. "He played 'Diego Delgado'. And after the police came in, I saw our real Delgado interrogating him with a look of absolute stupefaction on his face."

"Our Delgado hadn't realized he was getting his fifteen minutes of fame that night."

"So then did Gonzalez, as 'Delgado,' join the

crush around the jammed zipper?" I said. "Neither Lance nor Simone mentioned his name as being present."

"He wouldn't be getting his cue to come onstage until much later. He'd have no reason to be there in the wings," Maya said. "Unless he was doing something he shouldn't have been doing."

"But if he was hanging about backstage with no urgency, that might mean something to us," Cody said. "He might be the good cop gone bad, the killer in uniform."

"Have you seen that before, or something like that?" I said.

"Unfortunately, yes I have, but they never took as many bullets as I did on the force. They liked to be in on the action without having much of it."

"I can see," Maya said, placing her hand gently on his hairy wrist, "that the force is still with you."

CHAPTER NINE

I wish the force had also been with Maya and me on the following day. *May improvisation be with you* lacks the same impact.

Drew and Diana Carson, Rebecca's parents, already deeply grieving, must've have been additionally stressed by the trip down from New England, because they didn't call us until the morning after their arrival. I could understand that, since they would've needed to get their bearings, which aren't always easy to find here. Maya and I had kept our schedule open. She could've gone riding on Martina, her Lusitano mare, and I could've been painting, but it's too hard to concentrate on either with an impending but unscheduled appointment with grieving parents hanging over your head.

When Drew called he told me they were staying at a small, rather exclusive hotel with no more than a dozen rooms on a block long side street off Calle Hospicio. He stressed it was not a bed and breakfast, since it had a full staff. Had I ever heard of it? They preferred to meet us there rather than try to find their way around in a foreign country "under these conditions." They had found it difficult enough to get to San Miguel from that odd little airport in León, more than an hour's drive away, even though they had arranged a private driver. We agreed to meet them at the hotel at eleven.

Their upscale inn was located in a low-traffic area of *centro*, our quaint name for downtown, although the locals have called it that for 300 years. I remembered the hotel from walking past it a few times. A small cast bronze tablet near the door was its only signage. It read *el Escondite*, the Hideaway. People usually didn't notice it if they weren't looking for it, although I'm sure all the cab drivers knew it as an upscale destination. Drew and Diana could only have located it online. Maya and I walked over at about ten forty-five.

"This will probably require a lot of hand holding," I said, as we got closer. We'd easily ambled over from home on Quebrada. "You already know that."

"Of course. You'll hold her hand and I'll hold his. That's what we do best. I always feel I should've been trained to be a psychiatric nurse for this part of our cases." For today's meeting she had put on a pair of black slacks and a V-neck gray sweater over a white shirt with a collar. It looked very sober and even hinted at a semi-mourning tone, since the slacks were not nearly as tight as her usual spray-on jeans. Most of her jewelry was chunky mid-century Mexican silver, once skillfully but inexpensively made for the tourist trade. It was now highly collectable, but she hadn't worn any of it for this conversation.

My main concession to formality was to put on a denim sport jacket over pale olive chinos, but wearing the belt I'd bought in Oaxaca on an earlier case, with its erratic backstrap loom weaving, done in cryptic colored bars like campaign service ribbons on a uniform from a banana republic. I had also worn my good shoes, the Eccos made of real leather with no paint spatters.

When we walked into that tiny hotel, the concierge near the front door was less snooty than I expected.

"We are here to meet the Carsons at their invitation. We're from the Paul Zacher Agency," I said in what I thought of as my loftiest tone. I can do lofty now and then, and the elegantly appointed lobby seemed to call for it. Maya's subtle hand gesture to him said it better, if with a bit less refinement. Growing up in an upscale neighborhood in Mexico City, she has a finely tuned sense of class etiquette.

"One moment please. Have a seat if you will, while I see if they're in."

In to us, I thought. We might be meeting with the wrong class of people here. We have our own echelon of privileged people in México. We don't need to import any more from the north, where I've heard they are not in short supply, either. I paused to remind myself of what our visitors' mental condition must be after the loss of their daughter three days before. Maya and I walked further into the lobby and took a seat on a tufted black leather sofa.

The courtyard was surrounded by two upper galleries and open to the burnished late morning sky, although on one side I could detect the steel-framed edge of a sliding glass retractable roof; a wise precaution. Flowers were everywhere, and pots of marigolds ringed the upper level guardrail. Just after the end of the month we'd be celebrating Day of the Dead, and that flower was the traditional decoration. I was not tempted to see it as macabre in this context.

"Nice place," I said to Maya. "It has more of an international look."

She shrugged. "Not everything here has to be about tortillas and mariachis. This is probably where the Europeans stay. They'll have fresh croissants served at breakfast with tiny pots of jam and half-size cups of espresso."

"I wouldn't mind that now and then."

At that moment a couple walked toward us from the elevator bay. The man held his arm around the woman's waist until they were about ten feet away. She was wearing a buff colored straight linen skirt with a matching jacket. I tried to read them as the parents of Rebecca Carson. She had been small, not more than five feet tall, just as the real Mercy Buchanan was. In this couple, Drew Carson was the shorter one, perhaps five-foot-five, and Diana was closer to five-foot-eight. I knew this often worked quite well, even if it wasn't the typical couple's profile. The woman could always bask in the aura of having been an important catch for a height-challenged man.

Diana advanced with her hand out. It was soft and dry. His was moister with an attempt at strength in the grip. I struggled not to seem seven and a half inches taller than he was. Part of this business is trying to be relatable, especially for initial introductions.

"Thank you so much for coming out to see us on such short notice!" she said. "You don't know how comfortable we feel in this nice hotel, even if they don't seem to have much security. Maybe they do but it's not that obvious. I hope so. Anyway, it's like an oasis in a difficult place. And we didn't have a speck of trouble on the way in from the airport, either. To tell you the truth, I feel like no one knows we're here."

"I'm sure that's true," I said.

"I certainly wish we weren't here," said Drew Carson with an angry wave of his hand, one that seemed to dismiss the entire city, perhaps the country as well. He wore a lavender-blue and white striped shirt with a solid white collar, and khaki slacks with a sharp crease. His shoes were Dockers, although aside from our local reservoir there wasn't enough water to float a canoe within a hundred kilometers of where we sat. At least he wouldn't lose his traction in a puddle. His lips were slender and refined, as was his nose, and his hair was fine, thin, and blond.

"I'm sure," I said, "that after your terrible tragedy, security must be the highest priority when you pick a place to stay. Anywhere." I emphasized the last word.

"You do understand!" With a weary look Diana leaned over to hug me lightly around the neck. Her perfume was a blend that I had in the past encountered later in the day and under dimmer lighting. "You do know what we've been through, or maybe you can sense it, Paul. Thank you so much for your understanding. I know I won't ever get over this. It's going to be something I carry my whole life. We just have so many questions about how this could've happened. Perhaps you can tell us who we should talk to."

"Did you know our daughter well?" said Drew. Still frowning he leaned over to Maya as he sat down on a prim needlepoint chair nearby.

"Not at all, because we never had a chance to meet her. We weren't consulted in casting that play, or the writing of the script, and we didn't expect to be. We mainly gave our permission early on for the playwright to draw a case from our files, and then we attended the opening as their guests. Nothing happened for us between. What a tragedy that was!"

"What!" Diana Carson leaped up again. "You mean you saw Rebecca murdered? Is that what you're saying? You were right there? Didn't anyone try to stop it?" The shock and outrage dissolved and her face crumpled.

"We were in the front seats," I said, nodding gently. "Our partner Cody Williams ran onstage and reached her first. But there was no way she could've survived. I'm very sorry."

"I suppose no one even called 911," Drew said bitterly.

I shook my head. "Maya called an ambulance right away, before anything else happened."

"Did she suffer? Was she in pain at the end?" Diana slumped on the sofa, her hands clawing at each other.

I hesitated to say I'd seen other people die by gunshot wounds. To start making comparisons only underlined the horror of it. "To me, she appeared to die instantly. That's hard to tell you so bluntly, but my sense is, and I have some experience in these matters, that she would've felt nothing. She was simply gone. I hope that's a tiny consolation, as if anything could be."

"Of course, we can never understand exactly

how it was for her, will we?" Drew folded his arms and glanced around the lobby. "What I can't comprehend is how much risk she was taking just by coming down here to México. I can't imagine what she was thinking, not that we'll ever know now."

"Mr. Carson," I said softly, "I feel it would be a mistake to think this is in any way about México or its people. What I have found after solving a lot of cases in this town among both gringos and Mexicans is that trying to see any crime as a function of a given race or culture adds nothing to solving it. Crimes are committed by individuals in any society, not by a society in general, no matter how much people might wish to think that. That's just a shorthand version of reality that doesn't offer much help to us as detectives."

"Well, that's not what we always see in the papers at home, of course," said Diana, slightly more composed and knotting her hands in her lap with a gesture of subtle withdrawal.

"I'm very sure that's true," Maya said curtly. "So how can we help you today?"

He and Diana looked at each other before Drew spoke. "I guess what we wanted to know is who was doing what here to arrive at justice for our daughter. Mr. Fairfax has set up a meeting for us with Officer Delgado, is that his name? It's for later today. Of course the police here, who knows what kind of cover up they're going to offer us. But we wanted to meet with you first to get our bearings." He shrugged. "I don't know; maybe there's no point to any of this beyond identifying Rebecca's body."

"I don't know if I can even do that," Diana said, her voice on the edge of a wail. "I think the hardest thing in life must be to have to bury one of your children." She broke down and doubled over, her elbows on her knees as she covered her face and sobbed.

"Of course, there's no doubt about that," I said, after a moment. "It could hardly be any other way at this point. Diego Delgado will do his best for you. I can say that with confidence because we've worked with him on most of our eighteen cases before this one." I waited a moment for their response, but there was none. "By that I don't mean he'll act like an American cop, however, so you'll do better with him if you don't expect that. We'll also follow up with him and keep you posted on our progress and his, because Ken Fairfax has asked us to share any information we obtain with you. I likewise want to say how terribly sad we are at your daughter's death, and that we will do everything to support you by solving this crime as quickly as possible."

Biting her lower lip, Diana reached out and placed her hand on my wrist. "I'm confident you both will do that. I suddenly feel so buoyed up by the support of the Paul Zacher Agency when we're so far away from home."

At this point I knew that Maya had recognized the touchy-feely aspect of Diana Carson's character. This was common throughout México among women of every class, although only among their own class, and Diana would probably have been horrified to hear that.

"Do either of you speak some Spanish?" Maya said. "Licenciado Delgado does not have much English, and as a matter of pride, he often pretends to have none."

"We both had some in college," Diana said. "It's kind of faded now, I suppose. I do remember *mucho gusto* (glad to meet you)." She failed at her attempt at a chuckle.

"That will help." Maya nodded.

"Anything will help," I said.

Drew pursed his lips and spread his hands palm upward in an open gesture. "So what comes next?"

"I think the main thing is that we have established a contact with you," Maya said. "We are no longer names from a list to each other. We are bound together in a search for the truth."

I smiled, thinking that this sounded a bit too high-minded to me, but Maya could spin the web of a female spider high and wide when she chose. She had done it to me in the past. It was not that she was cynical, but she always knew what to say in situations that were burdened with strong feeling. As a Mexican, the scaffolding of her emotional life had a broader structure than mine did. It also ran several stories higher. Now, the bereaved couple was rightly searching for closure and justice. You couldn't blame them for being snagged in Maya's harmless but unavoidable web.

"We've already started interviewing the other actors and the stage personnel," I said. "It's going to take a while because there are a lot of suspects."

Diana gave me a focused look through watery eyes. "You feel sure it was not an accident?"

"Without being able to suggest a suspect or a motive, yes I do. Did Rebecca ever mention to you any contacts or relationships she had formed down here?"

"Well, she'd been gone now for about four months," Drew said, not looking directly at any of us. "She was in a frame of mind in early June that she was ready to take some time off from school, at least to not return in the fall, and she wasn't sure if she wanted to continue beyond that. When she left she made no mention of connecting with anybody here. We only kept in touch by phone every week or two. I don't recall any names that she mentioned. You can probably understand that she didn't tell us everything that went on in her life." He looked affirmatively at Diana, and she also shook her head.

"I guess we didn't always listen that closely to her, either," Diana said. "I can see that better now, in hindsight, of course. She knew we didn't approve of her coming down here, even though her Spanish was very good, since it had been her college minor and she'd also studied it in high school. I wish now we'd been more... more..." Her hands fluttered helplessly in front of her face, catching nothing. When her eyes closed tears leaked out beneath the lids.

"Was this her first visit to México?" I said.

"No, no," said Drew, "she'd been down here earlier for a couple weeks during Christmas break last year. You know how the kids like to get away then. Have you seen her apartment yet?"

"We haven't, but we've already gotten the address from Ken Fairfax," I said.

"How did your daughter support herself?" Maya said. "Were you sending her money?"

"No, Rebecca always wanted to be in charge of her own life," said Diana, shaking her head. "She had some money left from the college fund her grandparents started when she was a kid. She'd controlled it herself since her freshman year. She was majoring in finance, thinking, I suppose, to get into business in a company that had connections in Latin America."

"Was it a large amount?" said Maya.

"I don't really know, but she might easily have had around ten or fifteen thousand dollars left. Perhaps even more. We felt she didn't want us to ask."

"You'll be wanting to clean out her belongings,

to take some of her things back with you," I suggested. I didn't add that there were other things among her belongings they would wish to get rid of, and the choices that would involve.

"Yes, and Ken Fairfax said he'd come with us if we wished and they could furnish us with a cop too if we wanted one. I mean, like if we felt at risk going over there wherever it is. I don't know what kind of place or neighborhood it was where she was living. I shudder at the thought of seeing it now, I really do."

"I'm sure," Maya said.

"I would guess the police have already gone through it," Drew said, "whatever they do in cases like this." The dismissive wave of his hand suggested that anything they could now do themselves would be a lost cause.

"Please let us know when that happens," I said, rising as I held out my card. "When you set it up with Diego Delgado, we'd like to go along and see the circumstances she was living in. There might be something there that gives us a clue as to why she died."

"But would you really be likely to see anything the police had missed?" Drew said to me. "Please don't misunderstand me, but don't they have all the procedures in place to solve something like this?"

I had heard this before more than once. "Of course, but I'm a painter as well as a detective." That artistic ability to see things differently was what had gotten me into this business in the first place. I wasn't sure he found my response convincing, but he didn't pursue it.

"And there's been no thought that the woman who shot Rebecca was, well, guilty of her murder?" Diana said. "I mean, really. That's the first thing I would ask."

"Of course that's the first question that was asked," I said. "We're not that far into it, but the police haven't charged her, and if you had been sitting there in the front row, as we were, it's hard to see how she could've been any more than an unknowing agent in your daughter's death."

"And so she'll just walk away from what she did, I guess," Drew said thoughtfully, shaking his head. He took Diana's hand in his own. "I suppose she's a Mexican too." He made a helplessly apologetic gesture in Maya's direction.

"Not at all," I said. "Simone Garfield grew up right around the corner from you, in Rhode Island. Playing a Mexican character was a role she would've had to work at, so to avoid any disconnect they chose to make her an American in the play, as she is in life."

I chose not to add that Americans can be killers too, often with groups of victims, and there are many people here south of the border that are afraid to visit the U.S. because it's so unpredictably dangerous. Here at least, if you're murdered, it's usually for business or family feud purposes, not because you're simply sitting in a theater or an airport, or merely walking by. Here you are murdered for a reason, which can be a more satisfying way to go than merely being a random target.

Of course, I may be only speculating on that.

CHAPTER TEN

That afternoon I received a call from Diego Delgado inviting the Paul Zacher Agency to join him at the visit of Drew and Diana Carson to their daughter Rebecca's apartment the following morning at ten. He was in his high courtesy mode, given the distressed condition of the parents. Since his English was never more than meager at best, and he rarely offered to use it, I felt he had more than one reason for inviting us—because aside from our natural people skills with gringos, we were all good translators. He added that the parents had not asked Ken Fairfax to be present, although he didn't say why. Tortured as he was, Fairfax was probably happy enough to not be invited.

Maya called Cody and brought him in on the visit. Of the three of us, he'd always had the most highly tuned forensic skills, and if the police had overlooked anything at Rebecca's lodgings he would find it. I didn't feel the answer was to be found there, but I was happy to look. The clue that solved the case could be sitting in the open on the kitchen counter. Since any crime scene is like a book by a masterful writer, it needs to be carefully read for all the nuance it offers.

We met Delgado waiting in his black and white cruiser near the point where Orizaba intersects with the Ancha de San Antonio, and we followed him west into the San Antonio neighborhood. Rebecca's former digs were on a street called 20 de Enero, just a few blocks down and to the left. It was a distinctly mixed area, where cheap rents could still be found next to gentrified casas and new construction. The street life was often vibrant and occasionally chancy, but the residents probably didn't mind it, thinking of it as local color. As a painter, I knew this term quite well, and I had no problem with it either. Both objects and people can appear quite different in each other's reflected light.

Licenciado Delgado and his driver stopped in the second block and he got out, wearing a newish version of his brown suit series. This one showed little wear on the elbows and probably had no bullet holes at all, although I couldn't see the back. He made a point of shaking hands with us as Drew and Diana emerged from the back seat. Drew was gripping her shoulder.

"I am so happy now to be able to settle this crime for all of us," Delgado said with little bravado. As Maya translated this for them I couldn't help but observe that none of the rest of us smiled at his comment. He was carrying a small leather purse, and reached into the backseat of his car to pull out an official-looking cardboard box with a lid. On the narrow end the name *R. Carson* was scrawled in an italic script with the date of the killing. Diana and Drew both stared at the box with a strained expression. One of them must have sat with it coming over, and from their faces it might've contained Rebecca's ashes.

"We are all ready to settle it," Cody said with a neutral face, but still nodding firmly in encouragement. "Thank you for your great efforts so far." He could sling it just as well as Maya in the early phases of a case.

Handing the box to Cody, Delgado drew a set of keys out of the purse, unlocked the green steel door of a narrow single-story façade at the street. The property was not more than three meters wide. He replaced the keys in his pocket. As he pushed it open, Drew and Diana both stared at the door with a painful look, as if some ghostly appearance awaited us behind it. Every part of this visit was going to be a fresh source of agony, I thought. To the left of the entry was a *fruteria* shop offering plastic baskets of fresh produce at the edge of the sidewalk. On the right was a house of more imposing scale that was firmly anonymous to the street.

Inside the entrance a corridor with roughly stuccoed white walls on both sides was open to the sky. With no other doors along its length, about seven or eight meters further in, a garden opened to us. I heard the mumbled words "What a shabby place," from Drew. But when we reached the garden we discovered a charmingly planted inner courtyard with an old stone fountain, now silent. On the left side and the back, two casitas faced this tiny park at a right angle. A covered walkway fronted each of them.

Delgado led the way to the one on the back wall. The sun coming over the parapets bathed the garden in a brilliant cheerful light, but I don't think any of us were moved by it. By now our visit had taken on an almost ceremonial ambience. The center of the front wall of the back casita was faced with a long bank of windows in steel frames. I wondered if we were about to violate Rebecca's privacy, not that she would mind now. With a practiced twist of his wrist, Delgado unlocked the door and we followed him in. Maya's hand suddenly seized mine.

Inside, the arrangement consisted of a large living room with a circular dining table at the right end and a fireplace centered on the back wall directly opposite the entry. The kitchen was also at the far end on the right and open to the living room. On the left was a doorway leading to a bedroom with a bath. Three long strips of glass block skylights lit the living room easily. Others illuminated the kitchen and the bedroom. The beamed ceiling sloped toward the courtyard in front.

My first impression was that of a generic Mexican rental interior with a scattering of feminine personal effects. A local peasant shawl hung over the back of one dining chair. The seating group was the typical leather and slat *equipal* sofa with two matching armchairs fronting the fireplace. Two wrought iron floor lamps with parchment shades lit the scene. A couple of tourist trade paintings of children with bright faces graced the walls. They were better than most of that genre, but not anything you could look at for ten years without wanting a change. On the coffee table, a paperback titled *Lost Girl* was turned over open in mid-read. As the others surveyed the scene, I quietly closed it and turned it face down. No one but Delgado noticed me do it, but that was his job. I wasn't sure he had enough English to understand the title.

Delgado set the purse and the cardboard box on the dining table. In the center of the stained and scuffed leather surface a small cut glass vase offered us an assortment of flowers shaped like tiny lilies. They were wilted now and drooping. Maya picked it up and silently moved it into the kitchen. Delgado lifted the lid off the evidence box as she returned. The three of us from the Agency crowded around him. Drew and Diana stayed near the doorway as he pulled out all the objects inside and placed them in a row on the table.

"These were the things the victim had with her

at the theater," he said, speaking over our heads toward the parents. "You can handle everything, we've already brought the prints to our records." He looked over at them. "We now have her clothes in our evidence room. They can be released to you at any time you wish."

Uncertain she needed to, Maya also translated this for them.

As if prepared for this, Drew was shaking his head firmly. "We would like to donate all of her clothes to the Goodwill, or whatever it's called here. Including Rebecca's clothing that you have downtown and whatever she left in this place. We talked about this coming down. What would be the point of bringing it back home?"

"But I would just like to see what jewelry she had here, if I could," said Diana, quietly.

"I can handle that for you," said Maya. "Don't worry."

I didn't know of any Goodwill outlet in San Miguel, but on Cinco de Mayo on Saturday mornings several women ran active small used clothing boutiques, hanging the items on trees or nearby walls.

Aside from Rebecca's wallet, we found a few makeup items, three coins totaling twenty-two pesos (a little more than a dollar), a travel packet of tissues, a package of birth control pills, and a pocket mirror in a leather case. Her house keys from the purse were still in Delgado's pocket.

"But I don't see her phone here," said Maya. "We'll need to look at that."

"One did not show itself within the purse," Delgado said. "This is everything we found."

Cody took a long step closer. "Now I wonder if the theater has a policy of allowing no cell phones backstage during a performance," he said. "Ken Fairfax can tell us that. I recall they asked the audience to turn them off just before the play began."

I nodded. "That would make sense. She probably left it here before she went to the theater."

"That's easy enough to find out. Let me call her number," Drew said, stepping forward, suddenly coming emotionally alive and pulling out his phone. He rang her as we waited, listening. No sound beyond our collective breathing was audible in the casita. Cody had moved away and was standing just inside the entrance to the bedroom, his ear cocked toward the bathroom, and I waited at the edge of the kitchen. Suddenly Diana Carson sat down on the sofa and covered her face with both hands.

"She's not there anymore. She's not anywhere now." Her muffled tones broke the silence.

And neither was her phone, and that was what was giving me pause. Perhaps it was turned off, but why, if she lived there alone? I looked at Delgado with my eyebrows raised. There was no need to explain the importance of this to him.

He shrugged. "What the policy might be at the theater, we do not know this. But we asked for all her belongings at the night of her death and no phone came with them from the stage manager. That is all I can say."

"I don't like this very much," Cody said. "That phone has access to a ton of information."

"And the killer knew that, too," Maya said. "I think the phone might cast a lot of light on this case, but I don't expect we'll find it."

"Did she bring down a laptop or a tablet?" I said to Drew.

"I don't think so. I know her laptop is at home, but I haven't seen the tablet. It might be here too. She could get all her email from the phone, of course, and she was never a gamer."

As the conversation went on in a low key behind me, I stepped out through the open front door and dialed Ken Fairfax. He picked up the call right away, knowing, I suspect, where I was calling from. I didn't need to go through all the Mexican courtesy steps with him. "What is your policy with cell phones during a performance? Do you exclude them from backstage? We're here at Rebecca's casita with her parents and Delgado, and we can't find hers."

"No, we don't, although a lot of theaters do bar them completely. We try to not be that rigid if we can get away with it. The actors and crew all have to turn them in to the prop mistress. She checks to make sure they're turned off as they come in, and then she puts them into a set of pigeonholes with everyone's name on them. It's in the dungeon next to the prop cabinet. You might check with Alfonso on this too. As the stage manager he might have some thoughts on who had one coming in and who didn't. It would've only been a small detail, but he's supposed to be the detail guy."

"So as everyone comes in there are a number of times when she leaves the prop table and the purse with the gun in it in order to put their cell phones in the proper pigeon holes in the dungeon."

"Well, yes, but in the time it would take to drop off the cell phone and return backstage a person could hardly pull out the gun, insert a third live round, reset the trigger properly and replace the gun in the purse."

"All right, it was just a thought. Thanks." In my tour of the backstage area, because all those pigeonholes were clearly empty, I'd paid them no attention, only noticing that they bore the names of the actors and crew. But without knowing it, Ken had underlined something else for me. The pigeonholes were thirty feet away from the prop table, down five steps in the dungeon, and set back behind a shallow wall. With everything else that was going on, the prop mistress, Nicole Landfair, couldn't have watched both stations effectively, even young and alert as she apparently was. So while it may have been impossible for someone to add a bullet to the gun before the play began, the same was not true of a person lifting a cell phone from the pigeonholes and slipping it into his pocket. And added to this was the distraction of the jammed zipper.

The other thing this told me was that our next conversation would have to be with Nicole. I believed she knew too much. And if she didn't, she should have. Her ignorance (or voluntary blindness), if that was the case, could tell us something too.

I walked back into Rebecca's living room to find the situation had deteriorated. That was no surprise. From what I could see, Diana may have risen to receive a consoling hug from Drew and, from under the edge of the coffee table, accidentally kicked out a single Nike trainer into the space between the table and the next chair. As she recoiled, it lay there now on its side, loose laces stretched out from it as if reaching for life. Diana was weeping uncontrollably. Drew looked stunned and incoherent, helpless. I picked it up along with its mate and put it out of sight into the bottom of Delgado's cardboard box.

Normally Maya would've been the one to deal with situations like this, pulling Drew up short and consoling Diana, but to my great surprise, Delgado stepped forward and took Diana into his arms. She offered no resistance, in fact, drew him closer. Cody's face held a look of subtle shock. Mine did too. Delgado's expression, over her shoulder, said to us, *I can do this too.*

Detectives are necessarily pragmatists, although it seemed that Drew was not. I wondered what he did for a living. We in the Agency let it all go, happy for Delgado's supportive response in an impossible situation.

We started our own search. Maya took the bathroom, Cody the bedroom, and I took the kitchen. That was familiar turf, since I did most of the meal preparations at home. Maya had grown up with a cook who did it, so her range was more limited.

Judging from the sparse contents of the cabinets, Rebecca hadn't wasted much time with any dishes that required preparation. The trash held a number of packaged food wrappers; prepared items you heat in the microwave, and two empty wine bottles. The cooking utensils were well used and less than adequate for making a serious dinner. On the inside of an upper cabinet door hung a calendar. The three days of the *Identity Crisis* performances were outlined in a black felt tip marker there. On the square for opening night Rebecca had drawn a large exclamation point. I wondered whether, as we had, she felt she'd gotten The Call.

There was no landline phone, and no notepads or messages. No clues or evidence that I could see, even though Rebecca had probably microwaved her last meal there. The contents of the refrigerator were minimal and offered nothing unexpected.

From the bathroom Maya brought out a few pieces of jewelry and set them on the dining table. They were all silver: three bracelets and two chains with pendants, four pairs of earrings, all delicate in design and of no great value. If Rebecca had brought any rings with her she must've been wearing them onstage, but we hadn't seen them in Delgado's box. He found a clean plastic bag in the kitchen, swept the jewelry into it, knotted the end, and handed it to Drew.

Still, we found nothing that was of any assistance to us. The casita was the residence of a short timer, a young woman in transit, perhaps with her next move uncertain, depending on what developed with the people around her. The fact that she had added nothing to the furnishings that hadn't come in with her luggage underlined her lack of commitment to living in San Miguel long term. Maya packed Rebecca's clothing into her suitcase to take away with us in the van, along with the makeup and toiletries. She also picked up the shoes from the bedroom. Waving their hands in pained dismissal, Drew and Diana wanted nothing to do with any of it. We walked back out to the slate sidewalk on 20 de Enero with Diana clutching Rebecca's small purse to her chest with both hands as if it might easily escape. Delgado relocked the door at the sidewalk.

We said goodbye to them on the street. I didn't know whether we'd see them once more, but I told them again I'd keep them informed, whatever we came up with. Maya was towing Rebecca's suitcase. Walking away I felt like we were leaving a wake where we'd won the door prize, as if there could ever be one. When we reached my van I was still thinking about Rebecca's absent phone. Drew had given me the number.

As Delgado drove away with them we loaded Rebecca's suitcase in back and climbed inside. Maya had pulled the ID card out of the small leather sleeve on the top and slipped it into her jeans pocket. Someone on Cinco de Mayo would be ecstatic to get that suitcase full of clothes, but Maya and I would go through them first.

I paused for a moment with my hand on the driver's door. What felt like an informal memorial service had come to an end. Rebecca had made no more than a small impression on San Miguel, and the only substantial part of it had been the shocking manner of her death. It was hard to read any meaning into it, but I still couldn't stop thinking that at some level it must have one. I made up my mind that someone in the cast or crew would tell us what that meaning was, no matter what we had to do to wring it out of them.

It was only when I stuck the key in the ignition and adjusted my seat that I realized how angry I was over the tragic murder of Rebecca Carson.

CHAPTER ELEVEN

We had driven several long blocks down to Stirling Dickinson and turned up toward the Ancha de San Antonio before anyone spoke. The mood in the van was at once somber and speculative.

Cody wiped a fleck of dust from the dashboard with a blunt fingertip. He always sat in front because he needed the legroom. "Back in Peoria we always had to use the U.S. Marshals to crack cell phones when they came up in a case. It required a little preparation because we had to get approval from a captain to start that process. We couldn't contact the Marshalls ourselves until it had been set up by a higher authority."

"What did that get you once you got access?" I said.

"Well, it was a form of legal entrée, so you could use whatever you found in court. The email and phone contacts list would be on the sim card, so we do still need to find Rebecca's phone. The email and text messages should remain on the service provider's drive, but that's going to be a dead end unless we could crack her password."

Maya was nodding. "The San Bernardino terrorists proved that. Apple would never help the government crack their phone. Maybe they found a good hacker and did it by their own, I don't know. But I think all the Apple phone users were relieved that the company wouldn't co-operate, even in that kind of case."

"So with that precedent there is no chance at all of Rebecca's American service provider giving information to a Mexican police department, if they wouldn't even give it to their own government in a national security situation," I said. "It all hangs on recovering the phone ourselves. Are we up for a trip back to the Play House?"

It was still early in the day but I reached Ken Fairfax already in place at the theater. It made me wonder whether he was close to living there. As always he was eager to help us, but my first instinct was to not tell him why we were coming. "Trust no one," Cody has often said in the past. "Everyone is a suspect until you don't need any more suspects. Then you can speak freely."

Guilty people had engaged our services in other cases, as in the one we filed as *Jack & Jill*. Hiring us to see that justice would be done is one of the best covers for a criminal, although it tends to underestimate our capabilities. Not that I suspected Ken Fairfax of Rebecca's murder. Her death was too damaging to his current life's work, the San Miguel Play House. Still, the biggest lie is always the best lie, because it's so outrageous that people can't believe you'd tell it if it was false. They would say to themselves, "You could never make up something like that." Maybe I should stop thinking like that, or maybe not.

We found Ken in the lobby going through a stack of papers in the ticket booth. They looked like bills. "We took a big loss on this one, but not nearly as much as Rebecca or her parents, of course. If I could ever find a way of limiting my own risk and that of the people around me..."

"You'd be trading the stock market," Cody said, not unsympathetically.

"How did it go with the parents?"

"Difficult," Maya said. "In its own way it was like a memorial service for Rebecca. A quiet and respectful goodbye even as we packed up her things and took them away."

"Thanks for doing that. I almost went along, but then I wasn't sure if I'd be welcome. I hope you learned something useful, at least."

"I think we're getting closer to this," Maya said, resting her hand on his shoulder.

He looked up at her and his expression brightened. "What else do you need from me?"

Cody stepped toward him. "To some degree solving this could hinge on recovering Rebecca's cell phone."

"OK, but did you check the pigeon holes next to the prop cabinet? That's where they all are during the show. Maybe it's still there."

"When we came back the day after the murder they were already empty, so that told us nothing," I said, "not that we knew the phone was missing then."

Ken made a helpless gesture with both hands. "So at this point, I don't know how to help you with that. Nicole would know more than anyone. But I have to tell you that, for me, she's not a suspect in this. She would love to be an actor, but she knows she doesn't have what that takes, and being the prop mistress is as close as she can get to it. It's still an important role to play, and she can be part of the theater scene out of the spotlight and still soak up the atmosphere."

"We'd like to have another look backstage," Cody said. "We might've missed something."

Ken turned on the lights and led us through the theater. It was chilly inside and he wore a puffy black vest. The curtains that concealed the backstage area were open, so we could see that the stage was fully as deep behind them as in front. "Do you need to get into the prop cabinet again?" he said, pulling a ring of keys out of his pocket.

"No," Cody said, "but if you could unlock that

side door we'll take a closer look at the patio space. Since it was open during the performance there might be something out there." Our first visit had only been a walkthrough to check access to the street.

"Let me know if you need anything else." Ken opened the exit door for us and went back to the lobby.

In the dungeon the pigeonhole cellphone storage case offered twenty uncovered square recesses. All were empty now. On the lower edge of each was space for a name written on white tape to be easily changeable. The name spaces were blank but for two: Alfonso, the stage manager, and Nicole, the prop mistress, both in the bottom row. Cody lifted the box up and looked behind it, then shook it out over the floor.

"Nothing." He pulled at the prop cabinet but it didn't move off the wall.

"How likely is it that Rebecca's phone was simply misplaced?" I said softly, looking over the tools hanging on a pegboard next to the props. It was the usual display, hammers and screwdrivers, a drill with a steel box of bits, two sizes of pliers, a few chisels, and two small handsaws. A twenty-foot Stanley tape measure, four rolls of masking and electrical tape, and a trio of files in different shapes. Nothing seemed odd or out of place. I saw a few tools for handling wiring, an obvious need for setting up power on a stage. No cellphone had fallen between the cracks.

"I suppose we're a little late in the day with this," Cody said, pausing with his hands on his hips. "Anyone from the cast or crew could've come in here a dozen times since the murder."

We went up the rear steps on the left, paused on the landing that fronted the women's restroom, where Maya went in to check for the phone without success. Through the open door I heard her lift and replace the lid on both toilet tanks.

Out in the side patio the light was brilliant at that time of day and the space was marginally more inviting than when we came through earlier. The three big dead palm trees were still there in shabby round clay pots about a meter high. One had developed a crack and been reinforced with a rusty steel band. The space held no furniture and the ground was covered with rough-surfaced hexagonal concrete pavers. They had never been mortared between, so the margins were merely bare soil about half an inch wide that sprouted struggling weeds in a few places. The ten-foot stucco wall that enclosed the space offered a gate at the street with a rusty steel grill topped with sharp spikes. The impression was that it was no more than an emergency exit and hadn't been used for anything other than that in years. It didn't look like it was even part of the theater property, which was much better maintained, but more of an annex or an emergency easement through an unused lot.

"I don't know what we're going to get from this," I said. "The only place to hide a cell phone would be in the soil of those dead palms." I walked over and examined each of the pots. "All of this dirt is caked over and hasn't been disturbed in a long time. You can't fake that." The pots rested directly on the slightly uneven pavers, but there wasn't enough space to slide anything beneath them. Maya walked the periphery, silently studying the walls, occasionally reaching out to stick her fingers into a crack.

Cody was pacing off the enclosure, bent over and studying the surface row by row. When he'd gone through about two-thirds of the area, he paused behind one of the pots and dropped to his knees. One hand came up and drew his reading glasses out of his shirt pocket and his head quickly disappeared from view again. Maya and I converged behind him.

"This is interesting," he mumbled, doubled over about a foot above the concrete. "Show me the nearest window."

Pointlessly, Maya and I scanned the patio walls and the adjacent theater. There were none and we already knew that.

"No windows here, not even higher in the theater wall," I said. "Was that a trick question?"

"Then why am I looking at broken glass here?" He licked his index finger, touched the ground, and raised it into the undiluted sunlight above the rim of the clay pot. We both leaned in closer. On his fingertip we saw a dozen tiny glittering fragments. "And you know what else? Study their facets and they will tell you they are from a flat sheet of glass, not a tumbler or a champagne glass dropped at an opening night party."

"How thick is window glass?" I said. "I'm sure you would know that."

"In the States it's typically an eighth of an inch. They call that double strength. The next thicker level up from there brings in varieties of plate glass. Here in México normal window glass is metric and it's a little thicker than our double strength at home. I think it's about five millimeters thick and that's almost two tenths of an inch. Do you want to know what this glass on my finger is, judging from the fact that it's a sixteenth of an inch thick or even less? And tempered, I'm sure, but I can't tell that from this sample yet."

"Will you be speculating here?" said Maya, never an easy sell. Still, she was already pulling a small plastic bag from her purse to collect the samples from his finger.

Cody was accustomed to being challenged, usually in court during his days as a homicide detective in Peoria, so he was never indignant when it happened now. "Yes, I am speculating, but that's not the same as guessing, and this time it's well within limits. These, I believe, are the fragments of the screen of an iPhone that was smashed to bits out here, possibly using a hammer from the tool wall twenty feet away from us in the dungeon. How else would we find broken glass of this very specific kind in this unused patio with no furniture and no reason to be out here?"

"And nothing to celebrate," I nearly added. "How can we be sure it is that very specific kind of glass?"

"I'll send a sample off to my friends in the Chicago Police Department and they can test it in their lab. They'll charge us, of course. I'll run the cost by Ken when we go out. Now the question is, where is the rest of that smashed iPhone? And what else can we salvage from it if we can find it?"

"I'm sure it was taken away with the *basura*," said Maya, shaking her head. "By this time it would be mixed with tons of other trash at the dump. It's gone forever." In San Miguel the garbage trucks tour the neighborhoods three days a week. The local one on Avenida Independencia would've come at least once and possibly twice since the murder. The people who lived at the dump wouldn't welcome us rifling through their freshly deposited resources.

"But to be more certain, why wouldn't the killer have taken the cellphone away with him?" I said, "like in his underwear or in a sock? Then there would've been no residue like this for us to find, subtle as it is. He'd have more control of the evidence, since he could destroy it at home, risk free and on his own schedule. A clean getaway always counts for something."

"Sure, but what if the backstage people were being searched by Delgado's team as they left? The killer may have anticipated that too. Or if they weren't searched, he might've thought they would be, and what he thought at that moment is all that matters now. He didn't feel he could take a chance." Cody stood up and brushed off his knees as Maya took a clean tissue and swept as many minuscule fragments as she could into the evidence bag. "The killer wouldn't know what to expect, and having Rebecca's phone discovered on his person as he went out would've been a death sentence."

"Couldn't he have taken Rebecca's and left his own in the pigeonholes in her slot?" I said.

"That would be like leaving his calling card there for all the world to see. Delgado would've packed it up in that box and Drew and Diana today would've told us it wasn't hers."

"Because when Drew dialed the number at her casita that switched phone in the box of her belongings from the theater would not have rung," said Maya.

"If we'd found any reason to ask him to dial it as it lay there in front of us," Cody said. "That would've been a stretch."

"But you would've thought of that," Maya said to him, touching his arm affectionately, "eventually."

We tied up the minuscule bag of glass evidence chips Maya had so carefully collected and went back through the patio door into the theater. At least we had a sample of something we could work with. Aside from the murder weapon that was almost too obvious to be of any use, we'd collected no other physical evidence in this case. Of course, we hadn't yet gone through Rebecca's clothing from the casita. Delgado hadn't told us if he'd come upon anything else.

Next to the prop table now stood a green vinyl garbage can with a lid, lined with a black plastic bag that overlapped the edges. It was nearly empty. We'd had some success going through garbage containers before, but after two pickups from the garbage truck I didn't see any reason to pour it out.

I can't say that our visit was triumphant or even successful, since the evidence we had gathered was so much in need of support from lab work, but it still felt like a degree of progress. Interviews with potential suspects always have an abstract quality, but physical evidence is usually concrete and undeniable. We walked slowly, perhaps reflectively through the rest of the backstage area. It was uncomfortably silent, as if the scene was determined, as always, to yield nothing to us. I tried to see it as the hub of hushed activity it had been minutes before the murder, but it was too vacant now to help me call that up again.

I moved down five steps into the dressing room. Everything was neat and put away. In one of the cabinets I found the zip up hooded jacket 'Paul' had worn. I fingered the zipper but to my touch nothing remained of the jam. There were no irregularities in the metal teeth and it had not come from a fault in the bordering fabric, which was intact. Nothing I could see was changed among the other costumes. Maya was at my shoulder.

"If you wanted to, how would you cause that to jam?" I said.

She took the hooded jacket in both her hands, zipped it up six inches or so, and pretended to yank it apart.

As we passed through the mid stage line where the curtain would normally be drawn, I saw leaning against the column beyond stage left a single mop with its head partly draped over the edge of a bucket to dry. The floppy fiber arms of the mop head were brilliant red. The plastic bucket below was a light buff in color, an off-white shade near to a pale flesh tone. In that moment my first witness, the painter Bill Cramer, lost his credibility. This had to be the 'face' near the floor he'd seen at the edge of the curtain just before the second shot was fired. Had someone backstage inadvertently shifted the curtain slightly to expose the bucket at that critical moment?

CHAPTER TWELVE

This far into the case we had already been told too many times that we should talk next to the prop mistress, Nicole Landfair. While we always listen to advice of this kind, we are usually also desperate at this point in any case, so that made sense. Nicole had been in control of the fatal gun until it went into the purse of 'Maya', and less directly in charge of Rebecca's cellphone until it disappeared. She would've been the one to load the gun with two blanks (only). By now Cody had developed a steely glint in his eye whenever her name came up.

"I just know she's going to be some babe who is at the heart of this story," Maya said, as we drove away from the theater. "Trust me on that. The men are fighting over her."

"That's your typical filter on reality," I said. Maya's view of attractive women in our cases was well known to both Cody and me, so we took this with a grain of salt. That Nicole was twenty-six years old we knew from an earlier personnel inventory we'd gotten from Ken, but beyond that we had nothing other than her email and street address, and now, her commitment to talk to us.

Also on our list were Alfonso the stage manager, Rodrigo Ferrer, Del Rupert (as 'Cody'), and 'Delgado', acted by Ruben Gonzalez.

"How do we handle Nicole?" I said. "I think to have all three of us coming at her will be intimidating. We'll end up getting less from her than we could get by using only one or two."

"Then why don't you take it and just charm her sox off?" Cody said. Maya gave him a dirty look that he didn't see. She also pulled his ear to underline her point.

"Why don't you both go?" she said. "Then you can each charm her and get one sock apiece, but no one goes home with her. I'll go riding on my more predictable horse."

Cody and I both shrugged.

By email the appointment was set up for ten-thirty the following morning. When she responded quickly, the tone of Nicole's reply suggested she was surprised at how long it had taken us to get hold of her. With no visible regret or hesitation, Maya had indeed geared up with her breeches, boots, half chaps, and spurs, and gone out to Rancho Camarena in nearby Atotonilco to commune with Martina, her spirited Lusitano mare that had a weakness for Red Delicious apples and crisp carrots.

Nicole Landfair's address led Cody and me into the relaxed but gated community of La Aldea, entering west from the intersection of Calles Codo and Zacateros. It was a good location for people who wanted to be close to *el centro* and avoid hilly terrain. What it did not offer was a lot of smaller scale housing for young single people. The rather private homes were mostly family sized and the residents were mixed expats and locals, with some vacation homes for people from Mexico City and nearby Querétaro. The security was informal and the guard let us in with no discussion about our intentions. I had gotten inside without question before more than once, because our website designer lived there.

The address brought us to a substantial two-story house on a corner lot. It had been painted an elegant putty green tone. The window and door trim were made of rose-pumpkin colored cantera limestone. The effect was low key, balanced, and discreetly harmonious. You cannot assemble complementary colors with such flawless restraint by accident. As a painter, it struck me as far more sophisticated than the much too common run of ocher and blood red house colors here that were nonetheless colonially correct, from a time when much of the house paint was either made from dirt or blood, two much too common commodities at the time.

Cody checked the address again as I parked

down the block. "I wonder who we're dealing with on this round?" he said. He liked to speculate more than I did.

"Could Nicole be part of a big family? To me this looks like a lot of house for one person. How well could the job of prop mistress pay?" We had already talked about what a tough way to make a living acting must be, at least as hard as being a detective. After my first couple of years in San Miguel, my painting career had always paid much better than the Agency ever paid later. I took a covert satisfaction in this, since I also knew that most painters didn't sell enough pictures to pay for their paint and stretching new canvases. The arts have eternally been a challenging way to make a living. You always hear about the painting stars and their income in the millions, but for every star there are a thousand people close to *starving*.

"Landfair is a gringo name," I reminded him. "You don't see a lot of big gringo families here. Their reproductive tendencies have mostly petered out before they arrive."

We walked up the street and stopped at Nicole's door. It was constructed of a golden, varnished mesquite that needed to be refinished every three years, because the ultraviolet rays of the sun are not kind to clear finishes like that. "And who are we today?" I said, as if we were actors. Of course we always are. Cody had the best instinct for these conversations. "Are we doing the good cop or the bad cop roles this time?"

"Maybe it's both," he said. "Today you can be Othello, the man in a mixed race couple. That'll be all improvisation for you; you'd hardly have to think about it. I'll be Iago, the cynical betrayer in the plot and the creator of my own evil plan."

I shook my head. "Although I can see how that works, I think it'll be better if we're both here to be the good cop, eager to hear about Nicole's role in an important production of the local theater, and to get her opinion on who was where at the break, and who committed the crime. What did she think of our ingénue victim, Rebecca? Ken said that Nicole wanted to be an actress, but she didn't have the skills. Remember, we're also the real people on which three of these characters are based. Let's play on the credibility we can generate from that. And what if Nicole is the killer?"

I'd been thinking about this possibility since the moment of the murder, and even more as we walked outside the theater after talking to Delgado and his crew that first night. I had known about the job of prop mistress, but not about the person who held it at that time.

Cody paused in mid step and looked at me. "I also think she might be the killer, Paul, and I've thought that too ever since the first night. But if so, she'll tell us that, in one way or another. People can always control what they say better than what they show in their faces or their body language."

"So we're like the Inquisition, then?" I said, "gently probing her secrets?"

"Amen, brother. Let's start the fire under her stake." From his years of sessions in interrogation, Cody liked to begin like this.

The Mexican woman who answered the door was in her upper fifties. Her skin tone resembled a deep well-seasoned tan, her salt and pepper hair was pulled back into a perfect bun, and her immaculate floral apron had been freshly laundered and pressed.

I knew this presentation so well that I could've closed my eyes to describe it, or even to paint it. We were looking at the long-term trusted staff member in an upscale gringo or Mexican household, one who had by degrees earned her important place through dependability. She had done well enough there to be the main support of her own family, and judging from her age, possibly two generations of it. She may also have lorded it over the men in that family, who would probably not be earning as much as she did. But this was merely a collateral observation, since it told me nothing about Nicole Landfair.

"*Por favor, queremos hablar con Nicole Landfair. Tenemos una cita,*" I said. "She is expecting us."

"Of course. Please come in and I'll tell her you're

here." Her response could've been something we heard in a grocery store in rural Iowa.

"Why is her damn English better than mine?" Cody muttered to me behind his hand in an undertone as she led us inside.

We were standing in a wide high-ceilinged corridor fronted with three matching carved colonial mahogany chairs on each side. A long Persian runner covered most of the Travertine marble floor between them. The walls were paneled with more mahogany up to chair rail height, and wallpapered above in a subtly faded, aristocratic, floral pattern. I couldn't recall the last time I'd seen wallpaper in México, since the typical nubbiness of the plaster surface here usually doesn't allow for it. Edging the ceiling, the matching cornice was also mahogany. Halfway along the left side, a wide opening led into the living room.

"Don't be fooled by all this," Cody said, leaning over to me. "A lot of classy people are killers. Coming from money is always a great cover as they drive off in their Bentleys."

In the Zacher Agency case list we'd known several of those. I always read owning such a car as a mark of extravagant display, since the potholed cobblestone streets beat them up mercilessly, and you have to go to a different city to have them serviced. The guy that changed your oil would recognize immediately what a sap you were for driving a car like that here. His own vehicle, parked out of sight in the back lot, was a thirty-five-year old pickup, one that, while it ran impeccably, would never be worth more than eighty or a hundred dollars.

We walked down that imposing hallway, passing an unoccupied grand staircase on the right, and emerged into the courtyard, where I wondered if the house presentation and the brilliant sunlight promised more than we were going to receive from the coming interview.

"I wish it was always this easy," Cody said, shaking his head.

I wasn't as optimistic, yet I knew he enjoyed talking to privileged and entitled people, since they nearly always underestimated him. We sat down at an exquisite circular stone table veined in red and black with a thick rounded-over edge. Overhead a broad tan umbrella provided shade. After this introduction, I couldn't help thinking it was now show time for Nicole Landfair. Would she live up to the impression this establishment created around her? I realized I'd been thinking of her as a disheveled groupie hovering at the edge of the theater world.

It was a few minutes before she appeared. I glanced at my watch twice as I waited. Cody was sitting calmly with his hands folded on the table. Usually people were eager to get on with it, no matter what they expected from us. No one had come out to offer us refreshments.

Just then Nicole appeared from a doorway across the courtyard. She was a woman of medium height, wearing jeans and a loose bluish green peasant top that was mainly draped more than fitted over her shoulders. It made me wonder if she was hiding something.

"She's nervous," Cody said through his clenched teeth before she was close enough to hear. His expression dissolved into a standard smile as she approached. We both rose to shake her hand with slightly more genuineness.

"I'm so glad to meet you two after seeing the whole play in dress rehearsal! You were both so skillful in that case." The flip of her layered auburn hair I identified as grooming, always a defensive gesture, starting from primitive animals on up, one that means *don't attack me now, I'm doing something important.* I saw that Cody, who had nearly gotten a Ph.D. in psychology, had made a mental note of this too.

"So far we've talked to most of the characters in *Identity Crisis*," I began, "and now we want to get into the nuts and bolts of how everything happens backstage. We see your role as critical in that." Her initial uneasiness made me want to put more pressure on her.

"You think I know something." She gave us a sly smile. "Maybe I do."

"I'm sure you know something," Cody said.

"Only you may not realize it."

He was watching her with veiled interest as Nicole sat down across from us with a shrug. "Well, I don't know about that. As the stage manager, Alfonso was always the one with his fingers on the pulse of things backstage. The rest of us were only taking orders from him."

Where had we heard this *only taking orders* line before? The Nuremburg trials seemed like a harsh comparison, but the intent may have been the same.

"Excuse me if I get right to the heart of things, but we have been told," Cody said, with no special emphasis, "that the standard procedure in theater when there is a loaded gun on the stage is to have the person it's to be pointed at examine it before the play begins. Was that rule followed on opening night?"

Nicole had begun nodding vigorously halfway through this. "Absolutely. Both Alfonso and Ken Fairfax were present when I showed that gun to Rebecca with the cylinder turned out. She even looked through the barrel and said, 'bang', although the real point was to show her the two blank rounds as I put them into the cylinder. I felt she might have taken that moment more seriously. It was right after she came out of the dressing room, so maybe ten minutes before the play began. Believe me, everything goes by the book in a Ken Fairfax production." She was alternately looking us both in the eye as she said this.

DEATH IN THE THIRD ACT

Maya's prediction that Nicole was a woman whose appearance would cause any man's blood supply to quickly congregate in his pelvic area was somewhat off the mark. While she was perfectly acceptable in appearance, she was no natural beauty. She was more like the rest of us are; no femme fatale, no Byronic hero. She had a wide attractive mouth set in a pleasant but unremarkable face that would break no hearts, but could still find her a sound relationship with a loving man, if that was her goal. We had no way to guess what she wanted from life. My conjecture was that if she had high ambitions she wouldn't have been hanging around as a prop mistress at a small local theater. Was she expecting her break to suddenly come in the manner of *A Star Is Born?*

Still, for that hour of the morning, I found her makeup too perfect, too detailed, and above all, too carefully planned for her simple task of answering a few questions from two guys without any strong legal status in this case. She could have worn the same presentation to an opera in New York City without criticism from the upscale women in the adjacent seats. But for meeting two ordinary private detectives on her own turf in a small city in México, it brought three words into my mind. It was *way too calculated*, but why? What could we have observed in her face or manner if her presentation hadn't been so painstaking? This was a situation where doing nothing special to prepare for meeting us would've been less revealing and would've raised no flags.

"Then the real question," I said, softly, addressing her level of pre-performance care, "is how an extra live round could have been inserted into the cylinder of that gun between the time Rebecca saw it ten minutes before the opening curtain and the moment after the break when Simone Garfield fired it into her head." I was being intentionally more graphic than I needed to be.

Nicole looked at me for a long moment. The expression on her face was not as carefully prepared as her makeup had been. "It must've happened during the chaos," she finally said. "That's the only thing I can think of."

Cody leaned toward her over the stone table. His expression was still close to friendly but his eyes had grown stony. She couldn't read him as well as I did. "Isn't chaos rather a strong term for a jammed zipper, if that's what you're referring to?"

She shook her head firmly. "Normally it would be, but not if your cue is less than two minutes away. You can say what a small thing that was, a meaningless detail, but you don't know how it really is backstage. Trust me, I've seen the panic grow vivid in people's eyes; even with experienced actors when something like that goes wrong. No surprise is ever welcome. It's nothing you'd ever want."

"Was that jacket really necessary to the part?" Cody said.

"If Ken Fairfax thought it was necessary, then it was. Even if it was a jacket of his own that Lance normally wore around town, that's all that mattered."

"But can't most actors improvise in a tough spot?" I said. "Maybe grab one of those sport coats in the wardrobe locker?"

She gave me an informed look. "Yes, they can, but it's usually the last thing they'd choose to do. For a long time they've thought out their roles, and they'd always want to avoid having to reach out and make up something on the extremes. Besides, what they say is usually a cue for the next person's line, and you don't want it to be something she never expected from you. Improv is for comedians and amateurs."

"I have seen things go wrong too, on several cases," Cody said with a neutral expression. Was he seeing it now, in one of its lesser manifestations? "Often someone dies when that happens."

"There you are then." Nicole folded her arms and stared over her shoulder at a neutral cluster of sago palms.

It was my turn to lean across the table. "The key question here is who was present in the dressing room at that moment of chaos. Can you give me a list?" I pulled out my small, unobtrusive notebook.

Her eyebrows went up. "Well, if I can accurately recall it, because even if it wasn't totally chaos, it was surely too disruptive at a time when you need everyone to be serenely in control. Lance, of course, was there since he discovered the problem and it was his wardrobe change. He was the main one working on the zipper until the others crowded around him, but I think then he gave it up. I didn't see who took it. Alfonso had rushed over immediately. He had been standing close to the prop table directing traffic as we were getting ready to come off the break. Rebecca, of course, was there, and not far away from Lance, but she was mostly holding the sheet around her shoulders so she didn't get directly into the struggle to clear the jammed zipper."

"Who else?" I said. I didn't want to prompt her by offering any names.

"Well, I came over almost right away, as soon as I realized what was happening. I mean, they weren't making a lot of noise, naturally, since the audience was filtering back in. It was more like a suppressed murmur."

"Where was the purse with the gun in it at that moment?" Cody said.

"It stayed right there on the prop table. It was no more than a couple of minutes."

"Who else was in the dressing room?" I asked again.

She held up her index finger. "I'm thinking.

Earlier Rodrigo had been out on that side patio pacing back and forth. I know at first he thought he might go out and work the crowd in front during the break, but then he seemed suddenly a bit too shy to do that."

"What would the playwright normally do?" Cody said.

"I don't know. Although I know it happens, I've never been to an opening night before where the playwright had come. When the crowd first went out for the break, he told me he planned instead to talk to people when it was over. He wanted them to have a more complete impression of it."

"Like he wanted to explain why to you?" I said. "Did he feel it needed an explanation?"

Her hands fluttered. "Well, I guess he might've. It kind of seemed that way, as if he was bouncing the idea off me, or just trying to gather some courage. But you know, this was his first produced play, so he was vague about his role. Should he come forward and mingle halfway through, or should he hang back? Who wouldn't be in doubt?"

"I would be," Cody said in a tone of support, giving me a covert glance.

"Was the 'Delgado' actor there?" I said. At that moment I couldn't think of his name.

"No. His part comes only near the end, and while his entrance does include a gun, and I had one ready for him, the timing was nowhere close to that scene in the dressing room. And by the way, he doesn't draw his gun, either."

Indeed, the real Delgado's cue in life always came at the end, I thought. "Was his gun loaded with anything?" I said.

"No, since he would've never taken it out of his holster. That's another backstage rule."

By then I could see a name missing from this roster, a rather obvious one. Cody was ready with the question.

"When you rushed forward down the steps into the dressing room, was Simone Garfield already there trying to help out with that zipper? Think carefully before you respond." The old edgy Peoria Homicide Squad cop tone had entered his voice. It may have been in moments like this that he couldn't hold it back. It always signaled a tipping point when I heard it.

Nicole stared at the table for a long moment, her palms both down on it, as if the marble top had developed an awkward tendency to lift in a mild breeze that she'd never observed before.

"I want to say that she was, but the truth is that in a moment like that, a moment that looked like it meant nothing beyond a brief intense crisis that would quickly be resolved, I am not sure just where she was."

"One final question," I said. "Who killed

Rebecca?"

"Well, of course Simone did it."

"And did Simone add the live round to her gun?" Cody added as we both nodded.

Nicole shook her head. "I have no idea about that. In this scene we've been talking about I never looked back at the prop table, although it now seems like I should've. If you've been talking to the others backstage you know how chaotic it was."

"Did anyone else appear to be acting in any way that seemed suspicious to you?" Cody said.

Nicole folded her hands on the tabletop. "I have a vague kind of inkling about someone. I can't even say why, so I hate to bring it up. But you know how you can get a weird vibe sometimes?"

"Who is it?" I said, bluntly, not caring whether it was merely a vibe or a signed and notarized confession with three witnesses.

"Rodrigo Ferrer. He didn't come into the dressing room during the chaos period, as if he didn't want to be identified with it."

"You'd think he would be more concerned," Cody said. "He was very much into the detail."

"But he was still backstage somewhere, since he never went out to work the crowd as far as I noticed. At that time, he might've been out in the patio again, or still."

"Did you hear any special noise coming from out there?" I said. "Perhaps like a smashing or pounding sound?"

"No, but I wasn't focused on that either, not at all."

"How well did he know Rebecca?" My expression gave nothing away.

Nicole shook her head slowly. "I don't really know. I only had the impression that there was something going on, or that there had been in the recent past. It was like you could feel a vibration between them when they were in the same space, as if something unfinished was hanging in the air."

"Well, I think it's finished now," Cody said, slipping his note pen back into his pocket.

CHAPTER THIRTEEN

When Cody and I left Nicole at that handsome house in the Aldea community a few minutes later, neither of us was in an easy or contented frame of mind.

"So what did she tell us without meaning to?" I said after we got into the car.

"The makeup said she was carefully prepared for us, right down to the details. She had thought through what she felt we were going to ask her, and she had most of the answers ready."

I was nodding. "And she also wanted to draw our attention away from Simone without putting it on herself. How about her body language?"

"That kind of loose peasant style top reads as veiled to me, and although her jeans were snug, they're also neutral and universal. They tell us nothing more about her."

"She wore no jewelry."

"So she's not dressing up, but not dressing down

very much either," Cody said as we drove out through the gate and turned left onto Zacateros heading for our house on Quebrada to pick up Maya for a brunch strategy meeting at Aguamiel.

"What kind of person wants or needs to be that carefully prepared? Is she nervous about her role in the murder? Aside from all that business with the zipper, she still had custody of the murder weapon. That's the bottom line."

"That could be part of it, or maybe her preparation is just about being an orderly person with a solid planning function. I didn't pick up a lot from her, but for me Nicole is still very much a suspect. It's going to take more than one conversation to flush her out into the open, I think. I wonder who could characterize her relationship with Simone? Was there a rivalry of some kind there? Wouldn't she envy Simone's position as a lead actress if she had no hope of ever being one herself?"

"That's one angle," I said. "I also felt she was trying to shift some of the responsibility onto Alfonso. I suppose that's natural, given his role."

"He's a good patsy since he's automatically responsible for everything that goes on backstage."

"What if we catch her out in something that looks like negligence?" I said. "Might that get her to make a mistake as she tries to justify herself?"

"It might. Let me think on that."

Cody had called Maya as I drove and she was waiting for us on the sidewalk. It was a Sunday morning and Aguamiel opened for brunch at eleven o'clock. He had also called them ahead of time.

At Aguamiel the management always holds table #7 for us if they know we're coming in. At the rear of the front room, it's securely situated in a corner, so the three of us can all have our backs to the wall and face the door to the street, Calle Pípila. Not that we've ever had any trouble there, but you never know when one of our cases will bleed through into our private lives. It's a quiet neighborhood, and the restaurant is situated just down the slope from the southern face of the church of San Antonio. Like a lot of dining places in this town, it was once a private home, so it feels warm and intimate.

Over the years the Paul Zacher Agency has set up in several different restaurants for its working conferences. It was Tio Lucas for a while in the beginning, and then Harry's before it changed its name to Hank's, and after that a couple of others, including Hecho en México. Since they'd recently won the best restaurant award, we'd been holding our irregular meetings at Aguamiel. The proprietors knew us there, they guarded our privacy to the extent they could, and the bartender had learned how to make a planter's punch the way Cody liked them. Business is often personal like that here in San Miguel.

That morning the crowd was thin but building

steadily as Jennifer, one of the owners, ushered us to our seats. After she took our drink order and left us with menus, the mild buzz of the surrounding conversation covered ours.

"How was she?" said Maya. "As hot as you'd hoped?" Looking at me as she said this.

Cody adopted his even-handed moderator/negotiator tone. "Nicole Landfair was a normal person, a young woman of decent but not compelling good looks, well groomed with a careful demeanor, and she showed no sign of coming on to either of us."

"Not that I could see, either," I said, studying the other diners. A guitar player was setting up in the front corner.

"Her loss," Maya said, shaking her head. "She's probably guilty if she's holding herself back that much."

"On the other hand," Cody said, "I would've thought that if she was guilty she'd be all over us. Especially me."

"But she's not Mexican," Maya said with a gentle shrug.

"No."

"So the young Mexican woman suspect would be hinting at sexual favors if she was guilty, touching you constantly as you spoke, since that's another form of currency here," Maya said, "but the American woman would act standoffish and superior to you. Her chair would be pulled out a little from the table and her arms would be folded across her chest. Any suggestion that she was guilty would make her indignant. Her body language would forbid you to accuse her. Trust me on this, I've been around the block."

"A lot of the blocks here are very long," Cody said, looking around for his planter's punch.

"Half a block is often enough. I'm a quick study."

Maya had also made a long survey of English slang and vernacular usage. It was her principal hobby, after riding, which was more at the level of a passion. At that moment the waiter came with the drinks. Maya had lemonade made with mineral water and I had a dark Bohemia beer.

Cody delivered a concise recap of our conversation with Nicole Landfair, but one that emphasized the key details. "What's your take on it?" he said at the end.

Maya was silent for a long moment. "It seems there's something going on with her, but whether it involves her in the murder or it's only something that she knows, I can't make out. We need to draw her out more. Who's next in this round of conversations?"

"I'm thinking it should be Rodrigo," I said, "the budding playwright. I don't believe we know him well enough to understand his role, although we've all met him a couple of times."

"He was present backstage at the zipper crisis,"

Cody said to Maya, "but not nearby, according to Nicole. He didn't come into the dressing room."

"You might be recalling now," I said to Cody, "that Maya and I told you Diana and Drew said Rebecca had been down here before, earlier in the year."

"Yes, and I wonder if she and Rodrigo had made a connection of some kind then. I know we heard he had suggested her for the part of Mercy Buchanan, later called Rebecca." Maya raised her eyebrows as she said this.

"Then why would he want her dead?" Cody said. As this question hung in the air, as if on cue, the brunch dishes came. Maya had the eggs Benedict. Cody and I had the memorable *chilaquiles* tower with a side of bacon. This dish offered a subtle but endearing and tasty afterburn we both loved. After a moment, the chef, Gaby, came out to check our reaction. We gave her a series of high fives. I like it when the chef comes out to make sure she got it right.

"We're back to shuffling through the pile now," Maya said as she sliced into her eggs. "Is it Alfonso? Or Del Rupert, the Canadian who played 'Cody'?"

"I prefer not to think that," Cody said, drawing off the last of his planter's punch.

"Of course. But wouldn't that be a great cover for a killer?" I said. "In retirement, you've always been ready to commit whatever felonies we needed, mainly breaking and entering with those marvelous lock picks you carry around. I'm sure you have them with you now. Don't think we haven't noticed how it seems to balance out your career, gives it some artistic symmetry by weighting the other side of the scale with some serious felonies to counter all your good works."

Maya placed her hand on his wrist and rubbed it slightly. "You never give anyone a pass. Don't start now with that Canadian guy. They can be nasty too. I had a Canadian boyfriend once, briefly."

Cody could come up with no response. I hadn't heard about this episode either. Perhaps I would later, in bed, when she could sometimes be persuaded to talk about her earlier adventures, especially if we'd just had one ourselves.

"Anyway," Maya continued, with an unconvincing lightness in her tone, "we've still got that box of physical effects from Rebecca's casita to go through. I haven't been able to bring myself to do it yet. It's too personal. You both know what I'm talking about."

Cody came in with us when we got home. I was waiting for him to pull his latex evidence gloves on, but he didn't, although Maya had gotten hers out. Without forgetting about it, we had all been putting off going through the contents of Rebecca's prim green suitcase and this seemed like the right time. As I raised it onto the long table in the loggia all I could think about was how young she'd been at her death. An aura of cynical injustice hung over this case. Maya unzipped it and lifted the lid. She had quickly packed it in Rebecca's casita as we were about to leave, so she was no stranger to the contents in a general way, although she'd gone through none of it in any detail.

First we found two pairs of jeans folded neatly on top, followed by five or six sets of socks and underwear, all insubstantial, but nothing exotic. Maya, who could be the Queen of Sheba in bed, had a dislike of what she called "slutty" underwear. The toiletries were stored in one corner, including a hairdryer and a travel pack of tissues. We found a quantity of sunscreen, of course, because it was México, and more, because Rebecca had been a real blonde with vulnerable skin.

Cody went through all the pockets in the jeans and came up with nothing. In a zippered space along the back edge of the suitcase we found a wallet with a college ID, two credit cards and 1,400 pesos in cash—on that day worth about sixty-seven dollars. The peso had been sinking lately against U.S. currency and had slipped below a nickel in value. With it in that same slot we discovered her passport, a six-month tourist visa, and a Connecticut driver's license with a photo that, while it looked current, didn't do the dead girl justice. I tried not to think it had been her last picture.

Next in the clothing pile we found a stylish green blazer. This was not an item she could wear here every day, but suitable for a more upscale occasion. Maybe having that ready was a hopeful sign for her. Maya unfolded it and set it aside to lie flat. A pair of black slacks without pockets front or back followed. Two more pairs of shoes in little drawstring flannel travel bags. I checked inside all of them and found nothing. Half a dozen tops in solid colors, some with short sleeves, and some long, but none with pockets. Rebecca had preferred the cool tones of blues and greens. A sensible and prudent white flannel nightgown with a lacy collar—she had been here before, in January—in a pale blue flower print, and far from new. It must've been part of her comfort zone. I could understand that. México was not home for her.

I was hoping to find an unfashionable diary, one sealed with a chrome-plated clasp and one that would surrender intimate secrets to my inquisitive fingers, but as we touched bottom I didn't see one. Rebecca had kept it online if she maintained one at all. Perhaps it was an old-fashioned idea now.

Maya lifted the blazer by its padded shoulders and laid it flat on the table, where she went through the front pockets and found nothing. But from one of the two inside pockets she pulled out a letter still in its envelope, the top edge neatly sliced with a sharp letter opener, as if with care to cause the contents no damage. By the top corners she held it face up to us. Did people Rebecca's age write each other traditional letters anymore? Wasn't it now more about texting or email?

It was addressed to Rebecca at a college dorm. The stamp was Mexican and the postmark was dated March 14 of this year at Guanajuato, our capital city. The return address, in an elegant hand, read Rodrigo Ferrer.

"Well, well," said Cody looking over my shoulder. "Give me the testimony of physical evidence every time. This is where we call in forensics."

"As if you could," I said. "You know we'll have to turn this over to Delgado."

"Of course, after we copy and digest it."

Maya lifted out the two thin watermarked pages of text and spread them flat on the weathered boards of our table. The script had been done with a fountain pen using a fine nib and blue-violet ink. Without being florid or ornate, the fluid lettering was elegant beyond anything you were likely to see today, yet Rodrigo was hardly older than Rebecca had been. When I was in school they called this the art of penmanship, but I had no idea what it was called today. Maybe they don't even teach cursive script anymore. The only time I ever use it is when I sign a painting or endorse a check.

"Now we can see why he sent her a real letter," Maya said, with a sympathetic tilt to her jaw. "Rodrigo

Ferrer writes like an angel, and that artistic aspect is a big part of his message to her. This is an artifact she would always keep close to her, even if she later married someone else. Look where it was in her jacket." Maya pressed the two sheets to her breast for a moment and looked away from us, as if she were seeing herself in Rebecca's position. Perhaps she saw her own heart's journey reflected in this. The truth was, so did I, but neither of us wished to pursue it.

"But this is wonderful!" I said.

"And it's also what I was dreading." She spread it out again as we all bent over it. Rodrigo Ferrer had written this letter in English, as if that too was part of his sophisticated presentation.

To the dearest and best lady of all my whole life, my loving Rebecca, it began.

In that context, discovering this letter in a position where she would've carried it next to her heart, I think we all felt we'd been thrust from a murder case into a romance novel that, while it was classier than most, was still colored by a foredoomed tragic ending that had been worked out long before we arrived on the scene. As if on cue, we all looked away for an extended moment. This was Rodrigo's outcry in its most passionate form, well beyond the play he'd written for his MFA. Yet I felt, and I think the others did too, that we were also hearing, as a distant and fading echo of college age kids, the voice of Rebecca in response, now lost beyond that moment. Clearly the case now hinged on her reply and everything that followed between them, once she had returned to San Miguel four months ago.

Seeing that much, I decided not to quote any more of that letter in these notes, it was vibrant with hope and altogether too intimate. I usually don't care to violate the privacy of the dead, even though there have been times when we had to, as in the unforgettable case we filed as *Angel Face*.

Rodrigo's letter was clearly meant to be a private work of art for an audience of one. It was his eloquent appeal for her to return to San Miguel and take a place in the drama he had started to write. He would frame the role of Mercy Buchanan for her, even to the point of changing the real character's name to hers. Wasn't that a hook, and didn't he see it as the opening act of the coming drama of their lives? The style of writing had the extremely personal character of a young relationship that was already in bloom, but before it had encountered any pain.

As always, Rodrigo's unedited letter will be included in our complete case record if any qualified person wishes to research this investigation when it's finished. I'm thinking of filing this outing as *Death in the Third Act*, for obvious reasons.

"But now," I said, still looking away as we

composed ourselves, "the next scene will require the unhurried entry from stage left of the playwright himself, Señor Rodrigo Ferrer."

Cody smiled ironically. "I wonder whether it might be a big mistake to write your new lover into an important role? It may say more about who you wish to be than who you really are."

"And about who she really is, or was," said Maya, repacking the suitcase and dropping the lid back on. She zipped it from one corner to the other without encountering a snag.

CHAPTER FOURTEEN

Rodrigo Ferrer was clearly a stranger to writer's block, and he may have already begun his next play by the time I called him shortly afterward. In his entirely fictional sequel, if that were what it was, would he be able to revive Rebecca? And if he did save her, then from whose bullet was it? Delgado had told us the student playwright was still lingering in San Miguel, camped out with other cast and staff members from the state capital in a specially discounted bed and breakfast that would remain available as the case developed. By now, I was sure they were all pacing back and forth within those walls, snapping and pointing their fingers at each other, and perhaps knowing no more than we did.

Cody had gone home after we decided Maya and I would handle the conversation with the blooming author. At times our partner's physical presence could be too formidable to an artist with delicate sensibilities. Besides, Rodrigo had already shown a certain interest in Maya during our two prior encounters when he was trying to gauge the timbre of our vocal delivery as he tuned his script. For the coming meeting there was also a possible language issue, which I didn't think was much of a concern, since my Spanish is great, but Maya and Rodrigo were both native speakers, and if some trifling nuance came up, they would be able to resolve it instantly, as I thought then.

On his end, Rodrigo Ferrer picked up his cell immediately, made the normal required greetings, and asked how he could help us wrap this up. The touch of impatience I heard in his voice could mean one of two things. One, he was innocent of any involvement and simply wished to clear himself and get back to school. Or, two, he was hot to blame someone else and fade into the shadows. This would test my intelligence, something that happened every day. The detective business is not one where I ever expect to get any slack, and I don't.

Five minutes later we got a call from Diego Delgado asking if we really had scheduled an interview with Rodrigo Ferrer. When I admitted that we had, he said he'd release him from house arrest, or as he called it, *beneficial confinement*. This elegant euphemism made me wonder whether anyone had read the constitution here for a while. Of course, there had been many of them to choose from, so you could always find a provision in one that authorized what you wanted to do to somebody. México is a country that relies on precedent more than many others, and the repeal or overthrow of a prior constitution does not always diminish its lingering appropriateness for the task at hand. The history of government here illustrates a wide variety of possible ruling styles.

Twenty minutes later Rodrigo Ferrer was at our front door on Quebrada ringing the bell. Maya volunteered to let him in. As she walked away I could detect a subtle slinkiness in the tilt of her hips. It was always there to a varying degree, and it never went to zero, but this involved about a forty percent increase from normal.

When we had dealt with Rodrigo months before on those two interviews my impression was that of a grad student around twenty-four years old, earnest about the theater, and firmly articulate in English as well as his native Spanish. He appeared to have a well-developed sense of what he needed, and he asked intelligent questions. I tried to recall whether he had requested much information about Mercy Buchanan that he hadn't found in the case file, but this much later nothing stood out. At that time we had no cases going, and Rodrigo's visits bore no hint of setting up a coming murder. I was happily absorbed in painting and had a limited awareness of that developing theater project in any detail.

Maya emerged from the house with him hand in hand a moment later. It was about two-fifteen and I was already seated in the loggia with my small notebook and a pen on the table before me, a neutral investigator's expression on my face. Immediately I felt he looked different. It may have only been that the last time we saw him at the house there had as yet been no murder. Context always matters. We couldn't have regarded him then as a suspect for anything.

And why was he now? Did he have any reason to get rid of Rebecca? Had she arrived in San Miguel in possession of his rather florid but still eloquent and moving letter at an inconvenient moment, one when he was writing similar letters to another woman, or more than one? Six or eight? Was he marketing them online to other potential lovers that lacked his literary acumen? Had Rebecca only fallen into a net that had also trapped a dozen more ingénues? As we all sat down again after a series of normal greetings, I tried to reel myself in.

Still, I could see that Maya thought he was just too good looking. And I agreed. To me he would've been more relatable with some scar tissue on his face. Somehow I hadn't noticed this on our earlier encounters, when he didn't matter nearly as much as he did at this moment.

Let me be frank, not that I have to work at it. For one thing, I prefer to see dimples on men as part of a smile, appearing suddenly and unexpectedly, and then quietly receding as that smile fades into seriousness, but not permanently dug in on both cheeks for no justifiable reason. I'm not sure why I hadn't noticed this about him before.

"I want to thank you folks for getting me out of there," Rodrigo said with a radiant grin. Every single one of his teeth looked better than mine.

I also didn't think of Maya and me as *folks*—I could've stayed home in Ohio if I'd wanted to be thought of as *folks* as I approached my middle years, and I'd been surrounded by them there. Since I'd never been called *folks* in English by a Mexican, that use of the word seemed, well, too self-consciously *folksy*. Was Rodrigo now digging into the heart of midwestern idiom? Was he trying to become the new Thornton Wilder?

"Not a problem," said Maya with a shameless grin. "We're sad that you've been held in that bed and breakfast against your will while this goes on, but that wasn't our decision." I thought her chest might have swelled just a bit both in lift and projection as she said this, but then, she was well known for her ability to nearly raise the dead with her flirting. Privately I thought of it as the Lazarus effect. At least she hadn't offered to put him up in our guest bedroom until this charade was over. It's just down the hall.

"I'm absolutely sure you had nothing to do with that." As he smiled the cleft in Rodrigo's chin struggled for prominence with his dimples. I felt like puttying it up and painting it over. I have such a good touch with flesh tones. She's six years older than he is, I kept saying to myself, but I knew at this moment that meant nothing to either of them.

"The reason we wanted to talk to you again," I began, clearing my throat in a more resolute tone and with greater volume than I normally use, "is that we've been wondering whether you had a prior relationship with Rebecca." I didn't want to bring up his letter to her until I could observe how he was going to handle this.

"Of course you must have noticed her right away," Maya said, "when she first came down here." I wasn't sure where she meant to go with that. Perhaps only to say natural blondes tend to stand out in San Miguel.

I studied Rodrigo's face. After all, he wasn't an actor. He set his elbows on the table and hid his expression with both hands, as if he hadn't expected to hear her name come up so quickly. As I sat there studying his carefully trimmed fingernails I wasn't sure how to read his reaction.

"I'm sorry if that reopens a fresh wound," Maya said softly. I expected her to reach across the table and put her hand on his wrist, but she didn't.

"What I cannot bear," he said after a moment, "is that now anyone could think that I killed her, or arranged it. It's so not fair."

"So you two had gotten back together when she returned?" I said.

He nodded slowly, struggling to regain his composure. "Yes, and we had talked about getting married, even though Rebecca thought her parents might object. Well, OK, she was sure they would object. She hadn't told them about me yet."

"But in your mind marriage was definitely where you wished to go?" I said.

He nodded solemnly.

"I'm not surprised she felt her parents would resist that idea, given the way they feel about México," Maya said. "Had anyone else been in the picture for you before she came back to San Miguel? Someone who might have been jealous when Rebecca returned and connected with you?"

"I guess there have been a few others while she was gone, but no one important."

"Recently?" I said, trying to parse the varying degrees of meaning for *important*.

He looked up in surprise. "No! Are you thinking about Nicole Landfair? Ha! As if!" Both his hands spread outward in amazement. "Never, although she may have thought I was interested."

"Of course. But what would give Nicole that idea?" I said, smiling, as if the same thing inexplicably happened to me quite often, although it may have been a while.

Rodrigo looked at me solemnly. His jaw

tightened. It was time to get real. "I know you're not an actor," he said, "and I'm not either. But there are times as a real man when you have to play a role toward women that says, 'I'm flattered by your interest but I'm not going to respond. It's not about you.'"

"I have heard that happens sometimes," I said, quite neutrally. As a successful painter and an occasionally effective investigator, I didn't have much time to think about how a real man might act. In fact, I didn't even know what that term meant. Was there some kind of credential required? Was it the way you simply walked down the street? I could always look it up later online.

Do not go there if you want to live one more day, Maya's expression said in response. I gave her my best undimpled smile.

As I studied him I wondered how solid Rodrigo Ferrer really was. Of course in his current stressed and mournful condition, you couldn't see how he would normally act. I still wondered whether the playwright identity was only a role he played, but one he manifestly enjoyed. I'm always a little distrustful of credentials, possibly because my own is only a lousy BA in studio art, probably the most walked-away-from of all college diplomas, after sociology and political science. I've always managed to paint as if I didn't have one, because that degree has never added much insight or momentum to my process, which is thoroughly inner-directed. But similarly, why was a credential required for anyone to be a playwright? I had always thought that an MFA in writing qualified people to teach writing more than to practice it. Wouldn't it be the same in theater? It surely was in painting too.

I leaned forward across the plank table. Maybe it was only that Rodrigo was twenty-four years old, and many aspects of his character hadn't quite coalesced yet. Like all our cases, this situation was not going to bring out the best in anyone involved.

"Please tell me more about Nicole. Why would she think you were interested in her if you and Rebecca were contemplating marriage?" I had asked this once already in a slightly different form, and gotten nothing worthwhile from him. I tried to make my tone sound like I had just come up with this.

He looked down at the table, touching with his index finger something like a crumb or airborne particle that wasn't really there. Perhaps he was only trying to put his finger on the truth. But so was I, and I had done it before more than once with both hands in my pockets.

"At that time," Rodrigo added slowly, "I felt that Nicole looked at me as her ticket onto the stage. A career move, like a door was opening for her when we were introduced."

"What time was that?" Maya said pleasantly. Her chest had receded to a less demonstrative level.

"Earlier this year. She'd been the prop mistress at the Play House for only the last three productions. I had come down here from school to see a couple of performances. We have good theater in Guanajuato, but the faculty is strong on us seeing how things are done elsewhere in México. That was when I started getting things lined up with Ken Fairfax, and I spent a lot of time backstage. Nicole's job was to show me the layout and the mechanics of production in a real theater that wasn't part of a school setting. It was more than just academe because it had to be self-supporting. Ken had already agreed to help me if I could come up with a play that was worth producing. He had worked with my advisor on a production up in Monterrey ten years ago, and they were good friends, so that was an important connection for me. And I was sure I could write the play, if I could persuade you guys to give me access to your files." He said the last sentence for Maya's benefit.

"During that time what else did Nicole Landfair show you?" I said, trying to make that sound innocent.

His dimples faded to reveal a more vigorous jaw line.

"Enough to know that all I wanted from her was that she handle the props correctly when my play debuted."

"Was there something wrong with her?" said Maya, very quietly. She hadn't met Nicole, but she had heard the detailed report Cody and I assembled.

Rodrigo stared out across the garden, possibly at our rather tentative banana tree. It always looked droopy and apprehensive this time of year as if it could sense the chill of winter coming on.

"I am searching for the word now for the way she was being, or acting," he said after a pause. This was followed by a rapid scramble in Spanish directed at Maya.

"He thought she was needy," she said to me with a slightly distasteful look.

I nodded. "Needy in what way? What was Nicole looking for? Some kind of validation?" I knew a few people who judged themselves by the people they knew more than who they were themselves. They were always name-droppers. Maybe she only wanted to feel connected to something larger and more vibrant than herself. I tried to think whether I had seen any of that in her at our meeting.

Rodrigo's hands divided in what at first seemed like a welcoming gesture then quickly came back together. "More than that. What she wanted from me was to play the part of Maya." He cast an angular glance at her.

"And that part went to Simone Garfield," Maya said softly. From the slight crinkle at the corners of her eyes I could see she didn't care for this other casting idea.

"Did Nicole have some strong insight into that role?" I said.

Rodrigo shook his head. "She had none, or of any role, as far as I could see. I know she had approached Ken about doing at least one other part in an earlier play. He didn't use her."

"Were you interested in her beyond that?" I said.

At this juncture another language conference followed. I understood all of it.

"He thought she was what we would call *lofty*," Maya said, unnecessarily. I had caught the meaning quite well.

"Entitled," I said. "She would be offended if she didn't get that part, because she wanted to suggest to you that she deserved it even though she had no experience."

"Yes!" Rodrigo leaned toward me. "And I so quickly learned that other things could offend her."

"For example?"

It took a moment for him to respond. "She was offended when I connected so quickly with Rebecca on her first trip down here, earlier in this year. Her attitude to me changed."

I nodded slowly. "Can you tell us more about that?"

He placed his palms flat and unmoving on the table and studied the tiny open lines that divided the planks. "I met Rebecca early in January; she was only here during a school break. She told me she was getting tired of her college program and looking for something else to do for a while, although she was already signed up for the spring semester. She couldn't stay on at that time, although she wanted to."

"But she was hoping to get a better attitude with school later," I said to encourage him.

"Yes, I think so."

"So on the basis of that brief earlier trip, you and Rebecca decided to get married, but that didn't stop you from having other relationships before she returned. Did she find out about that?" He only stared back at me in response. Maya watched him with a somber look.

"As you consider that, I also need to know something else," I went on. "The others we've talked to can't place you at the end of the break when Lance's zipper was jammed, and I also need to know where you were at the moment Rebecca was killed. Lets get to the bottom line here, Rodrigo. This is the end of the last act for you."

At a muted belch or burp, Rodrigo's cheeks suddenly swelled out and a dazed look came over his face. He clapped his hand over his mouth as he leaped up and rushed into the garden. He skirted the mellow carved limestone fountain with an awkward twist of his hips, as if it had suddenly lunged at him in passing, although I'm sure it had rested there unmoving in that same attitude for two hundred years. I wondered if he was going to be ill. I started to stand up to follow him, but Maya put her hand on my wrist.

"Let Rodrigo find his own way back to us," she said quietly. "He'll return when he's able to talk again." I could only describe her expression as maternal, something I don't recall ever seeing before except in the presence of small children we didn't know. We sat there watching for a while as he stood panting under the taller of our two ficus trees, as if it offered him some shelter or stability. While his back was toward us, his head was bowed and his arms folded. His torso had a rhythmic motion as his chest heaved. As I stared at his bobbing form I was going over the elegant phrasing of his letter again in my mind. Contrasts like that can express the range of character in a suspect.

"What do you think now of Nicole in this?" Maya said, still surveying with a frown the developing situation under the ficus. I knew that Orlando, our garden grackle, was keeping his distance from this scene. Even as nothing ever got past him, he could still be shrewd in his choices.

I shrugged. It was not the true elaborate Mexican shrug, which addresses the weary overall condition of mankind, so amply expressed here, but the more focused detective shrug that says while you don't have enough information to respond to that question yet, you still feel the idea has some future potential.

"In a way, her role is almost too pat for me. I can imagine that like Simone, the shooter, Nicole might be set up here as a patsy in her own way. Isn't she a little too obvious as a candidate? It's like, well, she had responsibility for all the props. The loaded gun is a prop, so let's hang it on her. Then she may have been interested in Rodrigo for complex reasons. Not that I'm letting her off the hook, either. Cody and I both left her with the feeling there was more to be gotten from her, but neither of us knew what it might be."

"I know what you're saying, but I also hate to be thinking what I'm supposed to think. And that's the way it feels now."

"And what is that? That's why you're head of the Agency."

"That the killer, whoever it is, is a woman." She leaned back in her chair and gave me her most executive smile. If we could help it, neither of us was going to be fooled here. Not that we could always help it.

"We've run into some rough women here. They can be just as evil as men, sometimes worse. You know that." She didn't deny this, having occasionally pointed it out herself before I could.

Near the back wall, from the sheltered space between the ficus and the banana tree, we saw Rodrigo suddenly lurch forward and downward, his hands on his hips. An eruption of violent retching reached us. Maya stood up. "That would be landing right about on the anthurium," she said sadly. "You remember how much trouble we had getting that laceleaf to settle in last year."

I nodded. "We've never had to expense the replacement of an anthurium to a client before. Do you think Rodrigo needs some help out there?"

"I'll bring him some tissues, but this looks real enough to me. For Mexicans, mourning is mostly a private thing when you're among gringos."

"All through this case we've been looking at a lot of things as theater," I said, shaking my head as if we should rethink that. "It's hard not to. Who are all these actors we've talked to? Do they even live in the same world we inhabit? Or do they live in two worlds at once? Sometimes I don't know who I'm talking to."

"It's not my world, either," she said, with another long survey of the back wall, where Rodrigo was now standing upright again with his left hand braced on the smooth supportive trunk of the ficus.

Still, I could now see that the playwright's multilayered theater world in some ways overlapped mine, although not when I was involved in a case. As a painter, or I should say, an artist, reality was not my preferred field of operations. The uncomfortable connection to reality was happening out there now between the ficus and the reluctant banana. The result was a field sowed with doubt and hesitation, one of rough terrain full of stumbling and getting up again. It was a landscape constructed of unconscious fantasies, dreamlike figures, and information that left no trail from its origins. A condition where no verifiable sources existed, but that still invalidated none of them. This was the scene where Rodrigo had just discharged his current reality.

"Paul," Maya said. "Where are you? Come back to me."

"I'm still here, but approximately in the same way he is, I think. How much of this is real?"

"I hope none of it," she said as she rose to go out and bring Rodrigo back to us. "Normally you have a cast iron stomach."

CHAPTER FIFTEEN

A nd I do have a cast iron stomach, an undeniable asset in this business, so bring on the hot sauce. Rodrigo Ferrer was not in any condition to offer us more help after that, or to do more than barely help himself to stand without vomiting again, so I drove him home to his bargain bed and breakfast. Maya didn't come along with us, but we both knew another conversation, or more than one, would be required to establish his role in the death of Rebecca Carson. From the subtle curl of her lip, I could see that her goodbye to him had been somewhat less warm and cuddly as we walked out into the bright sunshine on Quebrada, although it was still polite. Her final farewell glance seemed to be searching for stains on his shirt.

I made a point of seeing that his window on the passenger side was fully opened before I pulled away from the curb. "I am very sorry for that," he said after we'd traveled about a kilometer. "I was suddenly overcome by sad feelings, and I felt it most here." As he placed his palm over his abdomen, his face looked puffy, almost rubbery now, with the dimples far less prominent.

I looked back at the traffic ahead. "I could see that. Don't blame yourself, Rodrigo." I didn't suggest he go back online and trace the profile of real man behavior. Manhood can take a serious hit if your entrails don't cooperate.

"I didn't know where the bathroom was in your house, and I didn't want to take a chance trying to find it."

"Of course. You made the right choice." For sure, as we used to say back in Ohio.

As I drove he stared at the side of my face for a while. "But I think I must be looking weak to you now."

I shrugged this off. Was this the man thing again? "Don't worry about it. I don't look at it that way. For me, true weakness comes from within your character, not your intestines or your sense of the ideal man. Grief can be physical; it can take any shape. But it's a passing thing, it does not say who you are, only what is bothering you at that moment. Go ahead and fall down and cry if you want. As a painter I can fall down any time. It doesn't make me weep, only gnash my teeth. But I always get up again. You will too."

"Thank you for that." He appeared to relax into the seat.

I let him settle for a while before speaking again.

"Could there be something in this you could use in a future play? Not the retching part necessarily, but the idea that grief or any strong feeling might have a direct and unexpected physical effect on one of your characters? I would give that some thought."

He gave me an almost startled look. "Thank you! I wouldn't think of that. You are truly an artist. Everything can be part of it. I know that now too."

"The ones who buy my paintings have said that. I only think that you can find your material anywhere, even in a scene like that, caught between the ficus and the banana."

He nodded slowly. "We have a saying here in México. It is this: Now you are between the sword and the wall."

"I have heard that from Maya more than once. But now you're upset, and you can better deal here with what remains of your distress. I think you're home now." I pulled up to the curb, as close as I could get to his bed and breakfast. We were about six car lengths down from the entrance.

He placed his hand on the door handle and paused. "What do you think of me now, Señor Zacher? I need to ask you this, please."

I turned to face him. "I'm not a judge, but I know you are an important player in this drama, and there will be a time very soon when we'll want to speak with you again to have those last questions answered. In that coming meeting I hope you will be more relaxed. And more forthcoming." I did not add that Maya would not be present to distract him, or herself.

His footing was a little shaky as I watched Rodrigo Ferrer walk carefully up the thirty meters of slate sidewalk to the bed and breakfast, unsure both of his performance and his morale. When he reached the door, he waved weakly as his other hand fished for the key in his pocket. Like I would do for any woman passenger of mine after dark, I watched the door close behind him before I pulled away. Five minutes later I was driving down Santo Domingo toward the Querétaro Road when my phone went off. Despite the narrow clearance I managed to pull it out of my pocket without veering into anybody coming up the slope. It was Cody.

"Paul! Glad you picked up! We've caught a break, but not for the victim. Alfonso Hurtado has been murdered."

"OK, but do we know him?" Still focused on Rodrigo, my mental wheels were spinning in neutral as I headed for *el centro*.

"We hadn't talked to him yet, but he's on our list. He was one of Rodrigo Ferrer's professors at the University of Guanajuato, and the stage manager for *Identity Crisis*."

"That Alfonso! I didn't remember his last name.

What happened?"

"He was caught in the parking lot behind that pharmacy across the Celaya highway from Mega and he was shot in the chest. I'm over there now with Diego Delgado and his crew. Where are you?"

"I'll start back up the hill and join you in a minute or two." I pulled out left instead of right and headed up the hill.

"Just come right on in. I want you to see the scene while it's still fresh. There's plenty of parking inside."

"I'm coming! How long ago did this happen?"

"Delgado says a little more than half an hour or forty minutes."

So, I thought, as I worked my way up the Querétaro road, this lets Rodrigo Ferrer off the hook, since he was with me then, unless he was part of a conspiracy, which I did not believe could have anything to do with the murder in act three. Or did it let him off? I wasn't ready to close out his file.

It was mid afternoon and the lunch break traffic held me back, but in eight minutes I reached the libramiento (our ring road) and flew down the hill toward the glorieta in front of the old Mega supermarket, now called la Comer. Across the street I pulled into a parking place near the front of the smaller of the two Farmacias Guadalajara. The ramp into the rear parking area had by then been blocked by a patrol car with blue and red lights swirling. No one was waiting in the driver's seat.

As I parked to one side and stepped out I called Maya to tell her what was happening.

The ramp led upward between the pharmacy and a walk-in clinic on the right. An officer in a black uniform and bulletproof vest stopped me near the top, but a shout from Delgado further in spun him around, and he waved me on through. At the upper level the site was an ell-shaped parking area, about thirty meters deep going forward at the rear of the pharmacy and then stretching to the right for another eighty meters or so behind the clinic and the adjacent buildings. Four cars were parked in the shallow leg of the lot and the murder scene was set up about halfway down on the longer stretch, where there were five more cars in a cluster. The group of half a dozen police included Diego Delgado directing traffic and barking orders. An ambulance idled some distance off, as if to acknowledge that nothing more than removal could be done for the victim. Under a brilliant afternoon sky the detail was sharp and unforgiving. What a gritty place to die, I thought. College professors were never immune once they got involved in this stark kind of reality. If "murder theory" was a subject, I have never heard about it, and I'd been involved in far more murders that anyone I know except for Cody and Delgado. As I walked toward them the heat was coming off the concrete pavement in waves.

The landscaping was minimal on both sides of this setting, with a row of five fledgling trees offering small pools of shade along both edges. There were no fences to the west or the north where the pavement ended, so the killer could have simply walked away through some rough open terrain and disappeared. I turned and looked back at the buildings for a moment; neither the clinic nor the pharmacy offered a rear or side entrance. This made sense; both would have a drug supply on hand.

Cody came over to meet me as I approached.

"Well, this one got away. I so wish now we'd tried to contact him. I remember seeing him onstage at the murder scene. Delgado says he was forty-five years old, an instructor in the theater program at the University of Guanajuato. His specialty was production."

"Then stage manager was the perfect job for him," I said. "This is not only just too sad, but it's thrown an entirely different light on this case. Anything interesting in this pockets?"

Cody shrugged. "We've only seen the wallet so far. Delgado's forensics people will go through the rest when they get him to the morgue."

We stopped between a recent Nissan sedan and an older Ford pickup. Delgado was talking with the medical examiner and didn't immediately come over to us. On the concrete the dead man was lying on his back, arms outstretched. One was extended flat along the pavement; the other was upright from the elbow on against the grubby front tire of the pickup. The face was calm, the eyes nearly closed but for an eighth-inch slit that looked out on nothing more. There was a considerable flow of blood running over both sides of the body from the bottom of his sternum.

A strip of small white stones set into the concrete neatly separated the parking spaces from one another. One of these lines ran under the victim's left leg and emerged from beneath his right shoulder.

"With that much blood I'm guessing the bullet hit the descending thoracic aorta," Cody said. "It would've bled out very fast, just like we're seeing here. Then the flow would stop when the heart stopped pumping. He died quickly."

A white cabbage moth innocently rounded the pickup in a flutter and hovered over the body. Was it drawn by the dark red of the blood?

Cody's insights, while often too graphic, are always on point. Like a mute witness, nearby beneath the trees stood a steel drum lettered **ARENA** (sand), but it was full to overflowing with white plastic bags of garbage. I took a step back.

At scenes like this, too often I imagined my own death. It could happen at any instant, just as this one apparently had for Alfonso Hurtado. In that version of those final moments I was usually framed in a semi-heroic pose with an expression of mild surprise, but certainly not shock. In scenes like this I always had enough time and presence of mind to utter a memorable last phrase, although it usually came out slightly off point. Especially when I viewed this prospect in my dreams my last words were often inappropriate, so I won't repeat more than one set of them here, as an example, addressed to Maya.

"Did you turn off the oven, darling?"

Read that as a practical take on existence, but it also makes me think that death, on arrival, mostly seems strangely inappropriate to life. We have no context for it, and it mainly resembles an exit door where and when you least expected to find one opening into your path.

"That's a damned down and dirty way to die," Cody said, shaking his head with a grim set to his jaw.

And Cody, I suddenly realized, must have contemplated something like this for himself as well, and more often than I had in the course of his long career in homicide. I suddenly recalled that he had been shot in the thigh on our first case, the one we filed as *Twenty Centavos*.

Suddenly Delgado turned to join us and delivered an edited version of his standard series of greetings. For once he didn't mention the progress of his two sons enrolled in that same University of Guanajuato, but in the law school division rather than theater. From the parting of his hands I sensed he felt he owed us an explanation.

"Of course, you will be quite soon to say, Señor Hurtado was in our custody as the police of this city. And who can blame you for asking this?"

"But you gave him a pass," Cody said, neutrally. "Probably a medical pass." The sweeping wave of his hand took in the setting, particularly the rear part of the pharmacy.

"Thank you for understanding this. When we have these...suspects in a case, all staying in the bed and breakfast of my cousin to be available, it is still not like a *carcel* (jail), do you see this? For example, we also permitted the exit of Rodrigo Ferrer to visit you today. Not a problem, except for the more fragile condition of his return. But then, once again, we allowed Señor Hurtado to go to obtain the refill of his blood pressure medication, and it comes out like this. We unfortunately do not have the sufficient personnel to accompany him." His backhand gesture to the crime scene appeared to contain a note of bitterness.

"Tragic, indeed," Cody said. "We do understand, but as you say, you are not running a *carcel* for people who are presumed to be innocent. Did you pick up anything out here on the scene? Perhaps a shell casing?"

"No. We have dusted the vehicles for prints, but who knows?"

"So the gun probably wasn't an automatic, unless the shooter found the ejected casing and picked it up again. But usually the killer will be too much in a hurry to hang around looking for it." I said. "A revolver wouldn't throw off a shell casing. Any footprints?" I pointed to the wide range of open terrain surrounding the parking lot.

Delgado made a gesture of discomfort. "Well, as you can see, the soil here is rough and full of gravel. There were in fact hundreds of footprints, mostly partial and vague, since we have had no rain for a while. Do you know, Señor Cody, how it is to be too much full of evidence? More than ever you can test?"

Cody nodded in sympathy. "Or, most likely the killer simply walked over the concrete surface here and drove away after the shooting. Look at this layout." He pointed behind him. "Neither of these buildings have a rear exit. The city is full of fireworks at any given time. You cannot even figure out what is being celebrated anymore. A single pistol shot in sight of no one echoing against blank walls would make no impression here whatever. My guess is that the killer knew that and either walked or drove away in no hurry, attracting no attention."

"Did the victim still have his cellphone?" I said.

Delgado shook his head. "No. Of course, we have looked for this first."

"Was he robbed of anything else?" Cody said.

"We do not think so. He has 1,600 pesos in his wallet (about $75 U.S.) and two credit cards."

"I would've taken his money and those cards," I said, "just to make it look like robbery, and to buy a good dinner for four later. Now we know the motive was something else." I studied Delgado's face for a moment. "When you questioned him on the evening of the murder, did you find anything significant in his statement?"

"Nothing that has stayed with me to this time, but I will email you a transcript of my notes later today. Who knows? There may be something there that has taken on more meaning now."

Again, the missing cell phone struck a chord with me, but I didn't want to bring up Rebecca's absent phone with Delgado present. He hadn't thought of it, and he didn't know about our glass fragment evidence from the theater patio. We were still waiting for the report to come back from the lab in Chicago before we gave it to him. As I stepped further away into the parking lot I heard no more from Cody or Delgado.

Walking out to the far edges of the lined spaces I surveyed the sterile rough-plastered back walls of a housing development going up two hundred meters away. At my feet, the dry crunchy soil would tell few tales, as Delgado had indicated. This was our first and only meeting with Alfonso Hurtado. What had he known?

And had that knowledge gotten him killed this

afternoon? One thing our Zacher Agency experience had taught all of us was that information can be very costly.

CHAPTER SIXTEEN

Cody followed me back to my house on Quebrada and we settled in with Maya in the loggia facing the rear garden. The time was coming up on four-thirty so I fetched a bottle of our normal Chilean working red wine, uncorked it, and poured a round while Cody brought Maya up to date. She was silent for a time.

"I know that Simone told us Alfonso was present in the dressing room during the zipper crisis," she said, "and as the stage manager, he would have good reason to be there. But I don't think we ever heard any more about where else he was during the intermission."

"Later he would've been moving around keeping an eye on things, I suppose, once the break was over," I said. "Then everything fell apart less than a minute later. As I look back now on that moment, I noticed that Alfonso was the one to reach Rebecca first after the shooting. I didn't know him then, but Cody and I both recognized him today. He pulled the sheet up higher on Rebecca's chest. I think he was moaning or muttering to himself, something like that. Delgado is going to email us the transcript of his statement."

"Motive will be the key to this," she said. "But how many motives could there be? What happened today behind the pharmacy was that Alfonso must have met with the murderer. The meeting was either planned, in which case he knew why he was meeting the murderer, or he was being targeted and he had no idea he was meeting anyone."

This was exactly the point. It could tip one way or the other.

Cody drained off the last of his wine and pushed his glass toward me. "The killer would have had only one way to know he was meeting Alfonso behind the clinic. We can be sure that he was not on duty 24/7 waiting for Alfonso to leave the bed and breakfast, when essentially, almost no one but the staff was leaving. It would've been a complete waste of time. Trust me on this; I've spent what seems like half my life on stakeout. It has a very small payout and waiting for Alfonso Hurtado to come out on his way to the pharmacy would've been even smaller."

Maya was already nodding. "That's how it looks to me too. It had to be already set up that Alfonso was going to meet the killer. People in the cast and crew would've had his cell number to set it up. But why wasn't he armed and ready?"

"Because it depends on who set up the meeting,"

Cody said. "If it was the killer, then maybe Alfonso didn't know that person did it, but if Alfonso set up the meeting himself, then he knew he was meeting the killer. This is why it would be so handy now to have his phone."

"If it happened that way, then he knew who the killer was," I said, "and that was his hole card. Did he hide that information in his room somewhere?"

"That way it would've been blackmail," said Cody. "That's been my theory ever since I saw the body today."

"Don't you think? Why else would you meet a killer?"

"Well, to arrest him, for starters."

"For a moment, try to think of this situation out of uniform," I said. "Alfonso may have been in a position in the dressing room to look up into the backstage area, like toward the prop table, and when everyone else was focused on clearing the snagged zipper, he could've witnessed the critical moment where the real bullet was added to the gun. From that distance, he may not have been sure what exactly he was seeing, but when the live round hit Rebecca, then he knew."

"Then what took him five days to come forward with his price for silence?" Maya said, never an easy sell.

Now Cody was again the old psychologist with an ironic smile. "How about this. One element was calculating whether he wanted to be involved in anything this dangerous. That's always the first thought. Two, what was it worth to the killer to walk away scot-free? If the payoff amount is too big, the murderer will simply kill again rather than pay it. Three, what damage would be done to Alfonso's own ethical sense of himself if he collected a serious amount of money to cover up the murder of an innocent young woman he had no possible grudge against? Most blackmailers are amateurs with a sudden good idea."

"One that often turns out not so good after all," I said. We all stared at the weathered plank table for a moment. I felt like searching with my fingertip for a single grain of sand on its surface, just as Rodrigo had earlier that same day, but I knew I would find no answer there either.

Three minutes later I was opening the second bottle of red near our desk in the great room when a message from Delgado came in on the Internet. It was the copy of his notes. I delivered the wine to Maya to pour while I went back in to the printer to make it part of the record. It was brief enough so that it took little time. The responses Alfonso had given Delgado at that initial questioning were no different that what you might expect. Where he was, what he was doing, what his feelings were toward anyone else onstage. Who did he suspect of switching the bullets? The answer to that was, "No one."

The only comment that appeared at all helpful

was that Delgado thought Alfonso appeared to be "nervous" when they spoke. This he did not elaborate upon. He closed by adding that no one at the bed and breakfast had heard Alfonso mention anything about meeting someone at the pharmacy. I brought the printout back to the table with a shrug. Maya scanned it and passed it on to Cody.

"So he was nervous because of what he already knew?" she said. "Or was it because he isn't comfortable with the police in any situation?"

That would not be unusual. The police throughout México are often regarded with suspicion and dread. Our own experience was different, but Cody and I hadn't grown up here. Maya had her own history growing up in Mexico City, but her father was a high official in the government oil company so his position may have provided some routine immunity.

"In either case it's irrelevant now," I said. "So where does that leave us?"

Cody pulled out his notebook. "We've got Del Rupert, the Canadian who played me, and Ruben Gonzales, who played Delgado, and the last one is Ivan del Toro who was Antonio Trujillo, the villain. But I didn't ever see Ivan onstage, and his part doesn't happen until the final scene, which was still some distance away when the play was stopped."

"Even 'Delgado' was not part of the action that

early," I said.

"Right. He came in about the same time as the real Delgado."

"Then Del Rupert as 'Cody' will be our next conversation," Maya said. "I think I'll take that one myself."

CHAPTER SEVENTEEN
MAYA SANCHEZ

I heard this morning that Alfonso had been murdered, too," said Del Rupert, AKA 'Cody,' still standing in the doorway of his house on the slopes of the Atascadero neighborhood. His lips were pressed so harshly together they looked crushed. "Nicole Landfair called me. I guess Rodrigo Ferrer is so upset he's about to collapse at any moment. Maybe that's no surprise, since he has a delicate constitution. Please come in. I do think it's fun to meet the real Maya, but not like this."

He shook his head as he led her through the house to a covered terrace overlooking a long narrow valley. Well-seasoned mansions and estates clung to both slopes with an air of being long settled before the wave of gringos had added 10,000 expatriates to the population. Across the valley on the left, a cluster of new houses or condos was going up that seemed excessively tall and almost arrogant; consciously, even intentionally, out of scale and tone with their surroundings.

It was the following day at two in the afternoon. Rupert had invited her for lunch when she called, but Maya politely refused, thinking it would be easier to get away when she'd finished with her questions if they weren't still eating. She hadn't met him earlier and preferred to keep Agency business separate from her social life. Her relationship with Paul would not have prevented her from having lunch with him had she chosen to, but that call was always up to her.

When Maya sat down at a glass-topped table, Del Rupert brought out glasses and a pitcher of cold water with ice. He was wearing a quiet pattern of a Tommy Bahama silk print shirt that hung out over his belt.

"I love the view from here, or I used to before they started that god-awful project. I'm going to put in a cluster of some Italian cypress on the end of the terrace; you know those real tall ones? Then I won't have to look at it anymore. Louise would've been so angry if she had lived to see it get like this."

Maya studied his face. Del Rupert was a broad man of average height with a wide face laced with a network of fine reddish lines. He must be a lover of wine, she thought. His hair was still thick and full, now turning iron gray, although his short, closely trimmed moustache was nearly white. She guessed his age at mid fifties. He did not remind her at all of Cody, his role, but she thought the casting was still plausible, given the limited number of actors in San Miguel.

"I'm sorry to hear that she passed away. Was it quite suddenly?"

Rupert gave a weary sigh. "No. She had gotten pancreatic cancer. It runs its course pretty much whatever they do. About three quarters of the way through it we didn't bother to go back to Canada anymore, it wasn't worth it. As far as we could see, the treatment wasn't helping and it was so difficult for her to be traveling that the doctor here just made her comfortable. She kind of drifted away." He smiled vaguely and nodded as if reassuring himself that had been the right thing to do.

Maya folded her hands on the table but added nothing to this.

He lowered himself into a chair opposite her. "I wish it could've been for her like it was for Rebecca. So fast, and probably so painless. Maybe that sounds like an insensitive thing to say because she was so young, but I still think a lot about Louise being so long in dying. I don't dwell on it, not all the time, of course. Would you like a glass of wine or anything?"

"No, thanks. It's a little early in the day for me, but feel free. Besides, I'm on duty now."

"I think I'll wait then too."

"Did you know Rebecca well?"

"I can't say that I did. She was a newcomer around here and I don't do that much theater work, although I do enjoy it when the right part comes my way. I usually play the guy the main character runs into in a bar and tells him all about his worries. It's like being kind of a foil that the others bounce things off of."

"I can see that. Did Rebecca or Rodrigo ever tell you anything like that?"

"No, I just never connected to them much. I'm sure you realize that in this play, I don't come on until Rebecca's dead, being Cody the cop. So I mainly saw her during rehearsals. She was a nice kid and very pretty, I thought." He cocked his head to one side. "A little flirty, I suppose, but at that age, you know how it is. I can't imagine that you're much older than she was."

Maya knew that at thirty, she was six or eight years older. She tried to think whether she'd been flirting at all with Del Rupert. She didn't think so, but sometimes it could be unconscious. While it had been a powerful tool in some earlier investigations, this was not the right moment for it. The problem was that flirting was so natural for her that it was hard to remember to switch it off at times.

"Have you played police roles before?" she said.

"Only in life, as you might say. My father was in the RCMP, a Mountie. I grew up in that culture. Not that it's any preparation for the theater."

She looked at him for a long moment. "What attracts you to the theater?"

He gave her an ironic grin. "The idea of making something from nothing by stepping outside of my sphere into the illusion of it all. As a Canadian I sometimes think I travel in a more circumscribed area than most Americans. I have a deep sense of the normal, of what's expected from me. Breaking away from that is fun. I like the idea of being Cody, although I haven't met him. Everything I know about him was in Rodrigo's script."

"There's no one like him. Did you gather any impressions about Rebecca's relations with the other cast or staff members? Was she especially close to anybody?" Maya was fishing for a connection with someone other than Rodrigo. So far the Agency hadn't turned up any real conflict among the cast or crew.

"Do you mean did I notice anything funny going on?" He topped off both their water glasses, hers first.

"Not just romantically, but perhaps was there any rivalry or animosity? I know from talking to other members of the production that there can be some rough edges in the offstage interactions. I only want to probe this a little further with you."

Rupert leaned forward over the table with a more intimate grin. "You know, Maya, your English is really good. I'm impressed."

Maya smiled sweetly. "So is yours," she said, leaning farther back in her chair.

He relaxed and his face took on a more focused

look. "I did wonder whether she might've had something happening with Rodrigo, but he was usually preoccupied when I saw him. He took a lot of pains with detail during the rehearsals, and since Rebecca didn't have one of the larger parts, that meant he was mostly interacting with the other actors more than with her."

"Did you see anything among those other actors, or even the prop mistress, that may have been a reaction to what you observed between Rebecca and Rodrigo?"

Del Rupert stared across the narrow valley for a long moment, resting his chin on his hand. High above, a lone raptor rode the thermals until it passed over their heads out of view. A frown slowly collected over Rupert's eyebrows. "Well, you know, there *was* one thing I saw that I thought was odd, but I let it go because I didn't catch very much of it. You need to understand that I'm usually working on my lines or my position onstage, so I'm not always that observant of what goes on around me offstage."

"Of course."

"Well, on that day, we were halfway through re-hearsals and I was just coming toward the dressing room with one of my own suits that I was going to use for the Cody part. I'd recently gotten it cleaned for the dress rehearsal, which was still about a week off, and I was going to hang it in the wardrobe cabinet. I heard two voices quarreling as I approached those stairs, and I pulled back just as I glimpsed Rebecca facing someone out of sight behind that short wall on the left. I guess I didn't want to get involved, eh? That's why I stopped."

"I do know how that is. Who was that other person she was talking to? Did you see her or were you only hearing her voice when you stopped?"

"I only heard the other voice, but they both were raised in anger. Rebecca was saying, or hissing, really–and I think these were her exact words, 'Don't ever try to pull that on me again!' The other person started to argue, denying something. I didn't catch it all, but it wasn't a woman Rebecca was talking to, Maya. That other person was Lance Bitman. Naturally we constantly tried to call him 'Paul,' since he always liked to stay in character."

A chill passed over Maya's arms and the small hairs rose on her neck. In her mind, the case suddenly rotated about ninety degrees. She had seen Paul's notes on his conversation with Lance, but now they took on a more sinister overtone. The actor had appeared to be playing games in the art studio interview, at least at first, but now that behavior appeared more deliberately veiled. By stressing how hard it had been to get a good read on Paul's character, Lance had also been directing attention away from himself.

Del Rupert's flushed face held a trace of minor triumph. He had made his point, playing on her assumptions about Rebecca's argument, and he had withheld the key issue of gender and identity until the last moment.

"Did you stay in that position to listen?" Maya said with a slightly cooler look.

"No. I didn't want them to notice that I'd over-heard part of their conversation, so I left before it ended and came back later to hang up my suit. At that time there was no reason to think it meant any more than a minor tiff between two actors would mean. Who could know what was coming? To tell you the truth, this production was minor league, like one in a college theater, and I was surprised that Ken Fairfax took it on."

"And you're sure they didn't see you?"

"No. I can move like the fog, invisibly." He gave her a satisfied smile.

Once again, I have been dealing with an actor, one who doesn't need to be onstage to be working, she said to herself as she rose from the table, pushing back her chair. This was another scene in the drama of his life, and I need to keep that more firmly in mind.

"Thanks for taking the time to meet with me," she said as she moved toward the door.

Holding onto her hand too long at the entry, he said, "Please let me know if you ever need anything else."

"Of course." She pressed his hand back for the briefest of instants and was gone.

CHAPTER EIGHTEEN

"At least Del Rupert didn't say he was at your service," I said when Maya returned and started her report as we took a circuit through the garden behind the house. She paused to survey the anthurium on the back wall. It was struggling after its assault by Rodrigo, but starting to come around.

"He would've been if I let him. I had the feeling he hadn't serviced anyone for quite a while. He would've been deeply grateful to me."

"I'm sure. Anyone would. But you weren't flirting with him."

"No. I didn't have to be this time. He was wearing silk for my arrival. In the kitchen he probably had a bottle of some great vintage French wine breathing."

"You're so standoffish."

"Not for you, but I do like to be off duty some times. Maybe later. I think I've got an itch somewhere."

"I'll find it." I called Cody to invite him to the conference.

"I don't feel like we're moving that fast," I said, as we awaited his arrival. "Sure, now Lance is the new hot suspect of the day, not to call your results trendy. Maybe it's only that the roving limelight has shifted to another character. We still have one or two left, like the guy that played Delgado."

"You have always hated anything trendy since before I met you. You're still wearing twelve year-old shirts with frayed collars. You refuse to eat sushi because everybody in California eats it and you think it'll give you a tapeworm."

"I know, I know." I brushed this away, feeling that being a painter allowed me to nurse a few eccentricities. "I'll get back to the Tuesday Market one of these days and get some new shirts. So then with Lance now looking like the murderer the crime becomes about rejection and revenge. A big ego trapped in a smallish boy's frame responding to a rebuff. But don't forget this, that during the great zipper crisis, Lance Bitman was at the center of attention nonstop. Among everyone, he had absolutely no chance to get away and mess with that gun inside the purse on the prop table."

"I know that, Paul, but what if that's not when it happened?"

"Yes, but I can't think of any other reason for that phony crisis."

"Anyway, I thought this over driving back," Maya

241

said. "What if Lance is *now* with Nicole?"

"OK." I heard my voice saturated with doubt, while hers rang with triumph. I've known for a while that I gauge the likelihood of liaisons like that by my own impression of the people involved. While that's neither fair nor very insightful, I still couldn't imagine Nicole being able to edge out Rebecca on her best day, but that was only my perspective. There was nothing very wrong with Nicole, but she lacked the spunky pizzazz of the murder victim. Or was money also part of this picture? If having serious money doesn't always make people attractive, it can, in this business, make them more interesting either as suspects or as the victims of suspects.

Maya continued. "When Rebecca said to Lance in that earlier conversation, 'Don't ever try to pull that on me again!' what if she meant trying to dump her for Nicole? She was the younger and cuter woman, one fresh and new in town, offering a bit of novelty within the small theater community."

"I wonder if that community gets bored now and then with its own limitations? I mean if you're casting, then there's always the same dependable but awfully familiar group to choose from. Budgets may not allow you to bring people in from New York or L.A. A new attractive younger person would have a real edge."

"You're suggesting Rebecca might also have felt entitled to Lance's attention."

"Exactly. You hit town and you check out the competition, always. Trust me Paul, I can take the woman's point of view on this so easily."

This had the ring both of experience and truth. "OK, and Del Rupert told you Rebecca was flirty. Maybe she was slicing a path through the males around her. But what about that letter from Rodrigo? To me, that seemed like the real deal. Where am I wrong?"

"Maybe he sent them out by the dozen. You saw how he looked. Maybe they were all the same letter with a different addressee at the top."

"But Maya, she had it in her jacket pocket, next to her heart. That says something about how she reacted to it."

She thought for a moment. "But almost any woman would cherish a letter like that, if it wasn't from some creep, even if they didn't want to start something with the guy who wrote it. Think of Cody always wanting to be with me. It's like that."

"It's a good fallback position. While he's not exactly waiting for me to die, if that should happen, he would know exactly what to do."

"Yes. Think of it that way." While I won't call Maya's expression smug, let's say it was reassured. Risk has always been a problem for her in this business. Having a good friend in the wings to shore her up made the risk more tolerable.

For me there was no argument there, since we all knew Cody had been in love with her for years, and this current slant added several possible new dimensions to the plot. At that moment the doorbell rang, offering the introduction of some forensic grounding to the discussion. Maya answered it and brought Cody out to the loggia. I pulled a bottle of wine out of the rack in the kitchen and three glasses out of the bar cabinet while she brought him up to date.

"Then we've got to go back to Lance," he said after I'd poured a round. "If, as I always thought, this is somehow about Rebecca's romantic entanglements, there could easily be more than one. Wasn't she entering a crowd? Doesn't that suggest multiple choices? As you suggested, Maya, what better way to establish herself here than to have all the theater men at her feet? The word ingénue once always implied naive, now it's only *apparently* naive. A woman's instincts can always run much deeper."

I took this up. "And isn't this case about appearances more than anything else? As you said before, Rebecca's murder was an act of theater. Almost everyone we've talked to is an actor, and I've felt almost like I've been onstage myself the entire time. Only I haven't read the script or attended the rehearsals. I'm like everybody's stand-in."

"No," Maya said, "I don't feel that, but at least

we lived the original case."

"Sure. But this is the sequel, and it's even more lethal."

"So here's how it goes now," Cody said, his hands fluttering over the table in general dismissal of all previous ideas. He always had an instinct for reducing the truth to its simplest elements. "We can say that Lance must have been initially attracted to Rebecca when she got the role because of Rodrigo's influence, and they started rehearsals. Rodrigo was around a lot, but busier than hell trying to get all the detail right. His role was that of Mother Hen, trying to get everything just as he had visualized it when he wrote the play. Most of that came from our case record."

"I can see him perfectly doing that," I said.

"And because he was not directing the play, he sometimes ran into a conflict there with this hugely experienced guy named Ken Fairfax, whose concern was shaping this fledgling scriptwriting effort into a real drama. Yes, Rodrigo was linked somehow to Rebecca too from her earlier visit, but what if now she was not getting enough attention from him because everything was about the production? She had come back to San Miguel with his letter next to her heart and it wasn't working out the way she'd thought it would, and it was too real for her. It didn't fit her fantasy at all. Didn't her parents say she was in an escape from school frame of mind?"

"You're making a lot of sense to me," Maya said, sipping her wine. "What then?"

"Miffed, Rebecca starts looking at her other options and she and Lance get something going," Cody said. "We don't know what exactly, maybe there's not enough time for it to develop very far, but then he sees another opportunity blooming in Nicole, who may have sensed this new rivalry. If she can't be a leading actress, maybe she can butt heads with one of them and take away her man. Remember what Lance said to you, Paul, that Nicole saw him as a way into more important roles in the theater, more than just the prop person. Maybe when he talked to you he put it all on her, but what if, while that may be true, it's only half the real story?"

"And then because he can't have both of them in such close quarters," Maya said, gathering steam from his momentum, "he tells Rebecca to back off, nicely of course."

"And Rebecca," I said, "both a lovely and a lively girl, has never been told before in her entire life to back off, nicely or otherwise."

"I'm sure you'd never tell her that," Maya said, folding her arms.

"I never met her face to face." I had a ready supply of proper responses. The truth was that I had known several women like Rebecca before I met Maya.

"Then Rebecca interferes somehow, with the new

connection Lance had starting up with Nicole," Cody added, "and the situation becomes too awkward for him to handle."

"I like it," I said. "I think he's too self-centered to have strong people skills. But we still have the problem of how Lance then adds the live round to the gun when he's surrounded by people trying to help him solve the zipper crisis."

Cody pushed his glass forward and I refilled it. He drank down a large draft and gave us a big smile. "That's why we call it theater, isn't it? What is it, if not illusion in every part of it?" We both stared back at him. "What if the zipper episode is a front designed to create the sense that the bullet was added then, and simultaneously giving Lance a terrific alibi?"

This was followed by a moment of silence. "Which it really does, I have to say. It is all theater, isn't it?" Maya said. "Even when we think were investigators, we're still just members of the audience."

"But," I said, with a solitary index finger raised skyward, "we're not regular audience members, we're acting as the opening night critics. And what we conclude from our attendance at this drama will determine this case's outcome. No one has yet seen the final act, even in rehearsal."

"Then we will write it ourselves," Cody said. "The upcoming scene is the one where Lance Bitman justifies himself or dies trying."

As I listened to him, I found myself taking a certain satisfaction in that outcome. What kind of actor was he? Creative? Spontaneous? Because the next act would be all improvisation.

"I hope you don't mean that literally, Cody," Maya said.

"You never know, do you? A lot of people believe that death comes in threes. Especially in the entertainment world."

Two down, I thought.

CHAPTER NINETEEN
CODY WILLIAMS

Once he returned to his condo on Prologación Aldama Cody scanned his email messages and found one from his contact in the Chicago Police Department. It stated informally that the glass fragment samples had almost certainly come from an iPhone 5. They had demolished one for comparison, but it was an older one and well used. He spent more time with the detailed report that was attached. It stopped short of stating how the phone had been demolished. This result came as no surprise, and somehow seemed less important now than when Maya had gathered the glass fragments in the uninviting patio outside the theater. Without adding any comment, he forwarded the report to Paul and Maya and stepped out through his French doors onto the shallow balcony outside where he dialed Lance Bitman's number. Two floors below, the modern fountain bubbled quietly and no one was present in the courtyard. The eight other balconies he could see were also empty.

On the fourth ring someone picked it up. "Star power here."

"Lance Bitman?"

"Yes. Who is this? Do I know you? Not everyone has my number."

"I'm sure. This is Cody Williams from the Paul Zacher Agency."

"I saw that name, but I've already met with the principal of that firm, sorry. I answered all his questions, so I have nothing more to say."

"Now you're talking to the principal investigator. Paul Zacher is just our lead scene painter. Once he's sketched in the background of things, then the senior team takes over. You probably talked mainly about playing him onstage. There's a lot more going on here behind the scenes, believe me." Cody had already examined the notes from Paul's conversation with Lance in detail and found no problem with it other than that there wasn't enough of it. "I'd like to sit down with you for another conversation. It won't take very long."

"Is this going to be about that stupid jammed zipper again? I thought that settled how the gun was doctored. Can't we get beyond that?"

"No. Why should we?"

An uncomfortable look crept over Lance's features. Cody couldn't see it but he could sense the deepening furrow in Lance's brow from the tone of his voice.

"I guess I assumed from the last conversation with your people that you think it lay at the heart of the mystery. I mean, you're calling the shots here, right, Cody?"

"I am calling the shots. Here's what I want from you now. Can you meet me in the morning at ten o'clock at Starbuck's?"

"The one on Hidalgo at the corner of the *jardín*?"

"Yes, that's the only one in San Miguel."

"OK. I'll see you then. I'll be the one looking like Paul Zacher."

"Right. Wear an artist's smock and a beret so I recognize you."

After he signed off Cody leaned back in his wicker chair. His long career had always been centered on watching people try to deliver one illusion or another. Often they announced their plan in advance, just as Lance had, as if by telling people what to expect they'd be more receptive to your lies.

In the morning Cody walked down Prologacíon Aldama at 9:30, skirted Parque Juarez, and climbed the short slope outside of the Hotel Sierra Nevada en el Parque. He walked round the corner to the narrow street behind it and waited in the shadows. He could see up Calle Recreo as far as the common gate of the apartment cluster where Lance Bitman lived. It was just past

La Parada Restaurant. Five minutes later Lance emerged into the street and turned right toward *centro*. Cody waited a minute before following him. By the time he reached the green painted wooden gate he already had his lock picks in hand and Lance was out of sight.

There is not much traffic on Recreo at that hour. It's only a single lane wide, and no one paused or even slowed during the sixty seconds it took Cody to get through the simple lock and slip inside.

The courtyard was strictly utilitarian with no serious plantings on the concrete slab. It offered parking for two absent cars. Two apartments opened to that level, and served by a single steel staircase, two more above. The one on the upper left, labeled C, was his target. He climbed the stairs silently and pressed his finger on the bell. The only window was a glass transom over the door. When no one responded he worked his way through a similar lock and was inside Lance's apartment in a little over a minute. After pulling on a pair of latex gloves he did not turn on any lights.

The space nearest the entry was laid out as a small kitchen with four single glass block skylights in the ceiling, and behind that a living room with a dining table, with a single bedroom and a small bathroom on the right. These two rooms were comfortably lit by pairs of windows facing north. The furniture was neat, well used, and unremarkable, but for a sleek black lacquered cabinet that supported a fifty-five inch flat screen television opposite the sofa. Everything was clean and orderly.

In the bedroom the double bed was made up. Cody pulled out the drawer in the nightstand and at first found nothing unusual beyond a couple of nasal congestion remedies, a clear plastic bag with three joints with a tubular wooden bead from a bead curtain, and a shoe horn. Near the front was a book of poems by T.S. Elliot. But as his fingers probed the back of the drawer they fastened on a clip holding five .38 cartridges held together by a brass strip that gripped them in a row by their ridged bases. Cody's pulse gained a few points as he put them back in place.

Now the clear target of his search was the gun that went with them. On the wall opposite the windows stood a tall armoire in rustic pine. There was no closet in the room. He pulled open both doors. The cabinet was filled to bursting with hanging clothes. He dragged his hand along their edges and detected nothing unduly heavy in the pockets. Pulling out the drawer at the bottom he discovered sweaters and scarves, and at the rear, a .38 caliber police special revolver that was an excellent match for those in the prop cabinet at the San Miguel Play House. He sniffed the barrel and found it had been recently fired. The cylinder held five live rounds and one empty casing.

This was obviously not the gun that had killed

Rebecca. Paul had displayed the presence of mind to recover that instantly onstage. But was this the gun that had killed Alfonso Hurtado behind the pharmacy? Planning to consider this in more detail later, he bagged the gun, zipped it into his left jacket pocket, and glanced at his watch. He still had eight minutes until he was to meet Lance Bitman at Starbuck's. This was going to be an interesting conversation.

The eighteen prior cases of the Paul Zacher Agency had demonstrated amply that the rules of U.S style evidence gathering do not apply in México. If you got it at all you got what you needed where and how you could. That was the governing rule. Warrants were either unknown or acquired later. All that mattered was what you came away with. If you violated the law in the process, it was up to the defense to prove that. The careful investigator in México tolerated no witnesses to his techniques.

Well within normal limits and not even on Mexican time, Cody was only three minutes late for their meeting when he sat down opposite Lance at the coffee shop. He was too agitated to drink any more coffee and he hadn't ordered one coming in. Still, he wasn't even breathing hard.

Lance watched him carefully, stirring his latte grande with a slender wooden stick. "I hope this is going to be worth it," he said finally.

"You have no idea how worth it this already is, *Paul.*"

Lance regarded him coolly. His expression, Cody thought, actually did resemble that of Paul Zacher, although only slightly. If nothing else, Bitman was a good mimic.

"Well, you've got that part right." He shoved his left foot out from the table to display one of the house paint spattered loafers Zacher had described in his report. Cody could not help but notice that Bitman was wearing the zip up hooded jacket from the play. He must have contributed it from his own wardrobe.

"The detective named Paul Zacher lives on in you today," Cody said, "although the play is finished. I'm so happy for that."

"And why does that make you happy?" Lance said with a trace of boredom in his voice.

Cody leaned across the table knowing he had nothing to lose. Either Lance knew it or he didn't, but either way his reaction would tell Cody something important. "I'm happy because here we're going to shift from illusion to reality. There's been another murder, Lance. Alfonso Hurtado was gunned down behind the pharmacy on the Celaya road across from la Comer."

There are readers and there are readers. With cheaters perched on the end of his nose, Cody spent a lot of time reading *Sports Illustrated*, but little in reading books, whether e-books or paper. His skill in reading people, however, surpassed all his other literary skills combined.

"I am deeply saddened to hear that. He was an effective stage manager," the actor across the table said to Cody, bring his hands together in an almost reverential pose.

"Possibly, but I can also see you are not in the least surprised. Who told you?"

The flicker of hesitation in Lance's eyes told Cody that the actor was now deep into the quicksand of improvisation, where nothing could keep him afloat but his own wit. This was Cody's home turf.

"Ruben Gonzalez." Lance could not keep the tiniest flicker of triumph from his face.

Gonzalez, playing Delgado, had had no chance to come onstage before the performance was cancelled. "He called you from the bed and breakfast to let you know."

"Of course."

"But how did he know about it?"

"The police had called the bed and breakfast. He was fortunate to pick up the phone in the courtyard."

"Who was calling?"

Lance offered an American shrug. It was not a deep comment on the fragile tissue of reality as shrugs normally are in México, but a shrug of simple denial, of avoidance, of flight.

"Did Ruben also say how Alfonso Hurtado was killed?"

Lance Bitman's gaze wavered for a convenient instant. He appeared to be studying the figure of a young Mexican girl walking by with two coffee cups in her hands.

"He didn't offer me that information, but it was a very quick call. I believe Ruben was rushing to an appointment at the time."

Cody nodded with great patience. "Possibly it was with his defense attorney. You might be thinking of calling yours now too."

"What?"

Cody reached into his pocket, pulled out the revolver in a zip lock plastic bag, and set it with a solid thunk in the center of the wooden table. With a gesture almost too quick to see, Lance spread his large paper napkin to cover it, surveying the other tables at the same instant.

"Now we can talk in more detail," Cody said. "I'm glad you were able to come today. I'm also happy to see you didn't have any trouble with the zipper on that jacket this time." Cody knew from the initial report of Paul's visit to the theater on the day after the murder that the dark blue hooded jacket had still been in the wardrobe. This meant that Lance had been back in the theater since then. Was that when he obtained the gun? And how did he get in? Cody couldn't see Ken Fairfax allowing him to enter and wander around the recent crime scene. The prop cabinet would've been locked too.

"How did you get this gun?"

"Simple. I let myself into your apartment on the way over here. That's what I do. Now let me ask you one. How did you get this gun? If I'm not mistaken it's one of those that were in the prop cabinet."

Lance covered the lower part of his face with his hands for a moment. "Nicole has the keys, not only for the prop cabinet but for the theater itself."

Cody gave him an appraising glance. "You must be close."

Lance shrugged. "We were briefly at one time."

"That's more than you told Paul when you talked with him."

"Well, as you suggested earlier, you're the chief investigator, not him."

"So give me the rest of it. The story of you and Nicole."

"It was like I told Paul. She thought she could be an actress. I didn't. She tried to find ways to persuade me. She started by giving me a set of keys as a gesture of goodwill. She said she'd given them to others too. It showed she had some power over what went on there.

Ken knew nothing about it. I thanked her and nothing more happened for a while. Then, quite frankly, she made me an offer I couldn't refuse."

"And you didn't refuse it."

"No, not the first time. But the second time I did. She still wasn't that good an actress, even in bed. Anyway, she thought I was more connected with Ken Fairfax than I really was."

"Aren't you?"

Lance looked away with an exasperated expression. "Ken would often rather cast someone else, OK? It's just that there aren't that many younger leads here, I mean under forty, and he has this rigid rule that he made for himself that he has to cast people within ten years of the age of the character."

"So you're one of too few choices."

"You could say that. The casting limitations of this theater scene are very often part of the decision of what plays to put on."

"I can see that." They stared at each other uncomfortably for a moment.

"Look, Cody. You're investigating a murder here. Now, two of them. There are a lot of deep feelings within this acting community and some of them are hostile. It can be a little like politics. People easily loose their sense of civility and decency sometimes."

Cody looked at him steadily for a long moment

without answering. Then, "Is that what happened to you? Maybe Rebecca found out about you and Nicole."

"Now I suppose you're thinking that I arranged the death of Rebecca."

"Might it be one more thing you *pulled on* her, Lance?"

Lance again avoided his gaze, this time muttering. He had entirely lost any resemblance to Paul Zacher. "That silly bitch! I knew someone would've heard her say that to me and then pass it on."

Cody first spotted the move coming in the corner of Lance's eye. His right hand was in motion at the same instant Lance's was. As the actor's fingers closed around the gun Cody's hand closed over his with much greater force. There was a sudden snap as if a dry twig had broken underfoot. With a bone in his index finger snapped, Lance's yell echoed through Starbuck's. Cody already had the disposable restraints in his other hand. He slipped them on Lance's wrists in a single gesture and dialed Diego Delgado.

CHAPTER TWENTY

O

f course it will depend on what Delgado's lab finds out about that gun," I said. "But I called Ken Fairfax and he confirmed that one of those house .38 police specials is missing from the prop cabinet. He had all the serial numbers and he gave them to Delgado."

"He must've been upset that there are extra keys out on the street," Maya said. "That's not his idea of running a tight ship."

"Right, and Nicole Landfair is now forever finished in this town as a prop mistress. Fairfax is planning to have all the locks changed next week, as soon as he can get the locksmith out there."

"But I wonder if all the damage is already done now," Maya said.

It was a rainy afternoon of that same day. October can be warm or chilly; it's hard to call in advance. Cody had just joined us in the great room where I'd started a fire. Over the mantel was my seated portrait of

Maya dressed as Frida Kahlo, right down to the unibrow.

"As for Alfonso Hurtado," said Cody, "as the stage manager he must've been in a better position to figure out what really happened to the bullets in the gun that killed Rebecca. I can only think he had an idea to blackmail Lance, and he paid for it. We know Lance still had the keys to the theater because he'd already recovered his jacket, which I think was rather careless on his part. Still, it would've been no big deal to get another revolver from the prop cabinet and buy some bullets at the Tuesday Market. Then he went to his meeting with Alfonso."

"There is an element of arrogance there, but we won't be able to prove any of this," I said somewhat sadly. "It'll be up to Delgado to sweat it all out of Lance."

"What if he can't?" Maya said.

"He's done it before."

"He's also been wrong before," she said.

"We all have," Cody said. "We're about 89% right on a good day."

"Not bad," I said. "But I wish we had found Rebecca's phone, now that we know for certain it was smashed up in that side patio. What if it's still there someplace in the theater, waiting for Lance to remove it once the heat is off? Wouldn't it be easier to hide it in some nook or cranny rather than take a chance it would be found in the trash, which is what we always assumed?"

"The busted up iPhone case with Lance's prints on it would clinch it for Delgado," Cody said. "I wonder if we owe it to Ken Fairfax and Rebecca's parents to take one further look around the site?"

"Nothing to lose by doing that," Maya said. "I know I would feel better. Maybe it's been a little too easy so far."

"Of course we don't have a key to the theater, unlike most of the actors and staff."

"Not a problem for me," Cody said. "Let's have some late comida while we plan this in more detail."

We adjourned to the kitchen to see what we could rustle up. I was able to construct an omelet of sufficient proportions to sustain us as we planned how to break the law once again. The subject of involving Ken came up briefly, but none of us could offer him a good excuse for what we were about to do, except that we all felt we may not have already done enough. None of us wanted to say that, so it was better to leave him out of it. He would never know that we'd returned for the phone unless we found it. After eating, Cody returned home for a wardrobe change and to oil his gun.

We thought it made sense to come at night wearing dark clothes. Calling it commando style would've been too dramatic, but it may still have been that we all felt theatrical doing that. There had been a matinee rehearsal that day and everyone was long gone when we arrived around 10:30. We parked in front of an industrial building half a block down, between two distant streetlights.

That stretch of Avenida Independencia offered no buildings adjacent to the theater and few even close by. We had first thought to station a sentry, but the surrounding terrain offered little cover. Across the street was the theater's improvised parking lot, unpaved and uncovered. The best plan seemed to be to avoid it since it would suggest theater activity to anyone passing. Now that Lance was in the carcel, we felt relatively safe. None of us thought the murder of Rebecca had been the result of a conspiracy. It still looked like a romance gone terribly wrong. Most adults know how that can happen, if not usually to this degree.

While our faces weren't blackened, and we could still rationalize our actions far enough to suggest that our hearts weren't either, I still found myself a bit queasy at breaking into Ken's highly personal theater after the scandal of all the keys that were handed out as party favors by aspiring actress and part-time good time girl, Nicole Landfair. In the end, setting ourselves apart from her would depend on what we came up with, as it always did. We in the Agency are nothing if not pragmatic.

That's why it came as such a shock when Cody stood at the main entrance of the San Miguel Play

House, lock pick ready in hand, my flashlight illuminating the way, and discovered that the door was not locked. With a limp hand he pushed it open into the darkened lobby.

You can curse with joy or frustration, but this moment was distinctly mixed. What had suddenly become easy at the entrance might become extremely difficult inside. We paused for a moment and looked at each other in that chancy light.

"This will be a shootout when we get inside, trust me on that," Maya said in a soft tone between fear and determination.

While I knew Lance was in custody, I somehow couldn't contradict her. Getting these cases wrong is the number one cause of not being able to walk away from them.

CHAPTER TWENTY-ONE

Like our outfits, the interior of the lobby was black. I aimed my small penlight into our path, pointing it straight down and keeping my hand around it. While no one said a word, I know it did not seem possible to any of us that Ken Fairfax was capable of walking away from his theater with the front door left unlocked.

But for us what was the strategy here? It was still most likely an oversight, so we paused at the top of the right side aisle. Ken Fairfax and his insurance company were not paying us to back up his faulty memory.

The body of the theater was dark, but to the left and upward narrow strips of light came from the direction of the lady's restroom and the approach to the patio beyond, and also the dungeon below, where the prop cabinet was.

On the right a subtle glow came from the dressing room.

We didn't feel we could talk, only gesture.

Fortunately, we were all armed. I had seen Ken at an earlier meeting with the stacks of bills that had to be paid, and some of them must've been from the electric company, which takes no prisoners here.

Looking back on that moment, I think the silence was the worst part of it. If only there had been some noise backstage, the sound of props or costumes being ruffled through would've changed our entire sense of what we were about to confront. At least we all had our guns out as I switched off the tiny flashlight. If this was only about Ken Fairfax's carelessness, he was going to pay for it. Negligence was not a category we had billed for in the past, but we would soon be adding it.

When we reached the edge of the stage without drawing any reaction, Cody signaled us to split up. He would take the critical dungeon with its props, since he could still pick any locks that got in his way. Maya would take the lady's room and the outside patio if that door was also open, and I would take the dressing room. Soon they were both gone.

I flashed my light for a split second on the prop table as I passed, but it was bare of props or anything else. In the near darkness I skirted the back edge of the stage, tracking it with my right calf as I moved toward the dressing room steps. I couldn't see where they began until I was there. The floor fell away under my next cautious step and I paused. No sound came from behind me.

I took one step down, then another. From my earlier visit I remembered that there were five.

The meager light came from a single bulb at one of the makeup tables. The other one was not lit. That was the only light in the room but it was enough to reveal on the makeup table the wreckage of a cell phone. It was bent and curled like a wartime relic, as if it had been beaten into a hollow space with a hammer.

If there is something like sick triumph, that is what I felt at that moment. There was no reason for that ruined phone to be there, unless a killer was trying to collect it. One who had been interrupted by my arrival.

There was only one way in or out of the dressing room; the steps I had just come down. As I scanned the three pairs of wardrobe doors the small hairs on my back were standing up.

I didn't think to yell for help, perhaps because I didn't know how many we were dealing with, but I had no doubt someone was waiting for me inside one of those wardrobes. What else did he know? I didn't think he knew who I was, so it could be that he thought I was Ken Fairfax.

So my gun was out. I was about to turn on more lights, but I had made no sound so it wasn't likely he thought anyone was there. That would change the instant I opened one of the wrong doors, if I did. I cocked my head to listen for Maya or Cody, but I heard nothing.

They were being as careful in their silence as I was.

These wardrobe doors had no locks, only a half-round pull on each door. Inside I remembered seeing a magnetic catch, which would release with a tiny click when you pulled the door open.

I am right handed, so I stood at the last pair of doors on the right, the gun in my right hand facing the left member of the pair. I snatched it open, ready to fire. There was nothing inside but a scattering of costumes I didn't recognize. They were not from *Identity Crisis*. The small click the catch made on opening provoked no other result. Nothing was behind the right-hand door but two crutches and a cane.

A small vein started pounding in my forehead as I went next to the left end. If the person inside was thinking I would go down the cabinets in order, this might surprise him. Or maybe nothing would now.

Again with the gun in my right hand, I snapped open the left door of the left end pair. This time five stacked suitcases in two piles met my gaze, as if the current production took place in an airport. No one was waiting for me behind the right member of the pair.

This made it easy, but now the waiting person knew which door I was about to pick. I could've fired a round through it, I suppose, and more than one. They were only made of thin plywood in a hardwood frame. But while I was a seasoned investigator, I was not a jury or judge, even less an executioner. By itself, the smashed cell phone proved nothing. This could only be resolved face to face. Putting my sweaty hand on the same left door handle, I jerked it open.

I wasn't ready. Of course I thought I was, but I've gone through this since in my mind at least fifty times, playing it out again second by second, thinking what I could've done better to maintain control of that scene. Those revised versions mostly work best in afterthought.

The door was barely open six inches before a long curved sword slashed downward through the opening and struck the gun from my hand. It skittered away on the tile floor to a place I did not see as I leapt backward. The blade did not touch me, but instantly rose again for another strike. Behind it a violent swirl of black cloth rushed at me, the hooded cape I had originally seen in that cabinet with the curved sword as I walked through with Ken Fairfax on the morning after the murder of Rebecca Carson.

I must have cried out in shock as I stumbled backward, unarmed, but I didn't hear it. The cape was rushing at me again, and I went over backwards, landing against the chair from one of the makeup tables. Where the face should have been was the familiar Guy Fawkes mask, the grinning, malevolent fool we always see on the Internet as 'Anonymous.'

Somehow I got a grip on the back of the chair,

and shoved it in front of me to take the next thrust of the sword, which broke one of the braces between the back legs. I rolled away, over and over. The blade sliced through my shirtsleeve. I screamed something, I don't remember what, as the blade came at me again and again, shearing off more pieces of that small chair. Chips were flying.

"Stop now or you're a dead man! Freeze!" Cody's voice like thunder. Then Maya's voice screamed something in the background, I don't know what. Running feet and then a horrendous explosion near my ear. The sword was still coming, down, further down, but now without any force behind it beyond simple gravity. The mask and the cape fell at once to the floor along with the person inside.

I struggled to my feet, tossing the chair aside. A bullet had gone through the left eye of the mask. Cody pulled it away. We all gasped at once. It was Simone Garfield. The bullet had passed through her eye as well, but the other one was still open, unseeing. She didn't move at all. Maya pulled the hood down over her face.

"She said she could play anyone," Maya said.

CONCLUSION

I am making these notes in early December, not too long after Thanksgiving in fact, not quite two months after the shocking murder onstage at the San Miguel Play House. How difficult it is to try to sum up the obvious, and the passage of that much time doesn't help. Hundreds of times I must have said to myself and to other people that it's often hard to know what you're looking at here in México. Part of that has to be what we are expecting to see. The idea that Simone Garfield could shoot Rebecca Carson dead in full view of 145 people and no one would think she was guilty of murder is beyond all reason, yet that is exactly what happened.

So while we know that theater is illusion, here we have reality as the greatest framework of illusion of all. The picture of Simone's guilt that we had so easily read as betrayed innocence was able to deceive not only the audience, but also the police and the Paul Zacher Agency. We ought to have known better, because we'd all witnessed the truth and we had all just as easily denied the real meaning of it.

Perhaps wisely, Rodrigo Ferrer disappeared the morning after Simone's death. Delgado had ordered the witnesses released from the bed and breakfast. We could only speculate that she had been involved with him and was snared in the same emotional trap that had caught Rebecca. Delgado told me that a search of Simone's apartment revealed a large amount of paper ashes in her fireplace. None of it was legible. But on her desk off the bedroom he found a letter from Rodrigo Ferrer. It began in this way: *To the dearest and best lady of all my whole life, my loving Simone.*

That was all. Diego Delgado released Lance Bitman the same morning. I've seen this happen before and he never apologizes. It's merely part of the system here to be mistakenly arrested. The case against Lance was already faltering, since his gun was quickly seen to not have been the one that killed Alfonso Hurtado, the stage manager. Simone would've had the sense to get rid of the murder weapon after she killed him. As a wrap up to the case this all had an untidy feel to it, unlike it would have had onstage, but not all our cases are satisfying by any means. Perhaps Nicole Landfair, Rebecca Carter, and Simone Garfield would've said the same about romantic relationships. I wanted to ask Rodrigo the same question, but I didn't think we'd ever see him again.

I carry no bitterness that Simone Garfield tried

to kill me. In that situation there was nothing else she could do, and she had already killed twice. I don't usually come out of a case admiring the killer, and admiration is not what I want to express here. While she came up far short on simple humanity, yet what a dedicated, steely-eyed killer Simone had been! And what a stunning actress. What incredible conviction! She was ready for Broadway, or London's West End. She was our own Lady Macbeth with dimples.

And above all, what nerve! I wish I had gotten to know her better, but my final encounter was enough to leave me with a strong impression, enough so that I knew I could never forget her. Searching for a name to put on this case, as I wrote the file I was mainly thinking about *Death in the Third Act*, but maybe *The Gambler* would be a better choice.

Simone's last rites were too private to make anyone in town aware of them as far as the Zacher Agency heard. Ken Fairfax recalled that she did have some family here, but he didn't know them beyond glimpsing them once or twice in the audience. In fact, he added, he now wasn't sure how well he had ever known Simone herself, even after working with her on nine different productions. Yet for him, her talent had never been in doubt. He said he would've trusted her in virtually any role, since her range was huge. I offered no disagreement with this, but that phone conversation with Ken sent me back to my own conversation with her. Who had she been for that encounter? One more character, the leading lady framed for murder, part of her enormous range.

In the days following her death I spent some time trying to imagine her grave marker. I suppose this means I was searching for closure. Violent endings often deliver a sense of conclusion without offering any resolution; they are two different things. Certainly a tombstone provides that in a way few other things can. I imagined her coming to rest in a quiet corner of the expat section of the Panteón, our main cemetery. The stone tablet would be the standard arched top limestone, wider than it was tall, and about three inches thick.

Since it was Simone buried there, I also imagined a special feature, an embellishment no others had. Below her name and the dates of her birth and death would be carved in relief those two linked symbolic masks of the theater: comedy and tragedy. But in the lower right corner, much smaller and peering out from behind the edge of one of them with its sinister grin, would be the Guy Fawkes mask, the emblem of Anonymous. The mystical figure whose identity and intentions are never clear, but whose appearance on the scene always signals the need for extreme caution.

Let us end it there, because whenever I think of this case in the future, I know that image will come to mind.